RADIUS ISLAMICUS

ESSENTIAL PROSE SERIES 148

Canada Council for the Arts
Conseil des Arts du Canada

ONTARIO ARTS COUNCIL
CONSEIL DES ARTS DE L'ONTARIO
an Ontario government agency
un organisme du gouvernement de l'Ontario

Canada

Guernica Editions Inc. acknowledges the support of the Canada Council for the Arts and the Ontario Arts Council. The Ontario Arts Council is an agency of the Government of Ontario.

We acknowledge the financial support of the Government of Canada.

RADIUS ISLAMICUS

Julian Samuel

GUERNICA
EDITIONS
TORONTO • BUFFALO • LANCASTER (U.K.)
2018

Julie Roorda, editor
Michael Mirolla, general editor
David Moratto, interior and cover design
Cover Painting:
Julian Samuel, *Get Dinner Ready on 14 or 15 August*
Guernica Editions Inc.
1569 Heritage Way, Oakville, (ON), Canada L6M 2Z7
2250 Military Road, Tonawanda, N.Y. 14150-6000 U.S.A.
www.guernicaeditions.com

Distributors:
University of Toronto Press Distribution,
5201 Dufferin Street, Toronto (ON), Canada M3H 5T8
Gazelle Book Services, White Cross Mills
High Town, Lancaster LA1 4XS U.K.

First edition.
Printed in Canada.

Legal Deposit – First Quarter
Library of Congress Catalog Card Number: 2017960394
Library and Archives Canada Cataloguing in Publication
Samuel, Julian, author
Radius Islamicus / Julian Samuel.

(Essential prose series ; 148)
Issued in print and electronic formats.
ISBN 978-1-77183-254-0 (softcover).--ISBN 978-1-77183-255-7
(EPUB).--
ISBN 978-1-77183-256-4 (Kindle)

I. Title. II. Series: Essential prose series ; 148

PS8587.A3623R33 2018 C813'.54 C2017-907290-0 C2017-907291-9

For Michael Neumann

Contents

A mullah's prayer is different from a mujahid's

—Allama Iqbal

1

Retirement home, Pierrefonds, Québec, Canada; 13 Jumada t-Tania AH 1455

Couldn't be me, I haven't any sons. I have young followers, far better than having sons. My progeny will have sons and daughters—daughters well-trained in the sciences. I might've had a wife but I can't always remember. The letter I'm holding appears to have been written by a young woman or perhaps it's a son writing to someone here. Sunlight, shaped by the window, frames the words in a trapezoid.

> *... I hope you find this. I've made notes, just like you ...*

After replacing the letter, I finish my cup of tea, and then I get up and walk along a wide hallway toward my room.

Behind the plasterboard wall is a concrete wall and behind that is the French-Canadian weather. In between these walls, there are wires, pipes, and a telephone connection attached to a CCTV network. On one of the monitors, the night nurse saw an old man fall out of bed and hit his head on the bedside table. Last week, two of us died. I had chats with some of the dead—I mean before they went—during breakfast or at lunch or in our library of forty volumes. They die in uric splendor in this home for the well-off.

Old people nowadays are more robust than old people in previous eras. Certainly, we're better off physically than during the time of Mohammad (PBUH). Scientists have found ways to slow aging to a snail's pace, and they study markers which make going to the toilet bright as flowers.

A woman walks past, using the corridor handrails and a walker. She has a welcoming eighty-five-year-old smile, but her health is from that previous era, before the current medicines. Her eyes had, moments ago, jealously noticed me reading the letter. Does she remember the act of reading? The letter means I have been in touch with the world outside. She says: "Hello." The walls are jaundice coloured, so I look at the trees outside under the white sun. Her name is not Martha; I am sure it's Jennifer. I say, "Hello Martha." Outside, the water curves out to Rivière des Prairies and eventually into the Saint Lawrence. Martha leaves an odour of boiled Brussels sprouts. Except for the shrieking woman in diapers, it's quiet here. Not much talking. Some of us do talk because we are off our Halcion. Jennifer, thank God, worked with us.

My friend Anver and other counter-Christians are aging beside me. I'm here to see them, and myself, through to the *shahre khamoshan*, *el muckbura*, the *kubristan*. I worry that some of my friends will start telling people what we did. Anver is sitting on a red chair beside a window. He tells stories about our past, especially about our crossing the Atlantic Ocean after the events we created. The chair remains an even colour of red, despite the shifting sun.

He was an old-young man when I brought him into

what we did. This tradition is passed down through the ages from Palaeolithic times. Even back then, we had members who looked like part of the tribe but weren't. We acted independently, far more rationally than the long forgotten *Ha'sha'shin*. We had money from someone. Yes. But we still had independence of mind and the will to level the playing field. Now, almost the entire world has turned its back on us.

He reminds me how we flew, via the small organization, to visit a Third World dictator's helper to get the supplies; money was considered part of the supplies. The business models we had to work with did alter our vision of the world. We had angel investors with billions, not mere millions.

A few women on our side invented an Islamic Exchange Traded Fund which would be listed and instantly de-listed and then listed again—all nanoseconds apart—to avoid being detected by the Securities and Exchange Commission. Our index names: BAW (Bomb's Away Wahhabi); CUBA (Cultivated Urban Banchood Arabs); TAH (Terror At Home)—all traded on the TASE. Of course there was some religion here and there, but the religious material was not top on their list. The real battle was one series of equities competing with other equities set in an iniquitous value system—call it the stock market—that has been around since 600 years before Jesus Christ. The mamluks in the media made everything gloriously Islamic but it wasn't: it was about money and having access to clean water and drainage and enough black cloth on earth to cover all women head to foot; to cover all trees (their swaying in the wind could cause sexual ideas and images to emerge in the mind); all lakes and all mountains all covered in black cloth; the Milky Way covered in black.

We're sitting in the library in the home outside Montreal. I'm in a chair which is not as red as Anver's. With my hand actions, I pretend I'm showing him my passport. He looks at the travel document and looks at me, amused.

The sea enters his head and puts us in the middle of the ocean, a few days after the events we created. The sea is smooth now, but we've had storms during the crossing. Anver tells me he can see the curvature of the earth, even though we are in very low orbit. A group of geezers walk along the decks like spectral beings, not offending anyone with farts smelling of limp carrots, just walking. From his chair in the home, Anver tells me our story set at sea on a luxury liner. "Wouldn't you like to see just one more glassy sea at twilight?" I ask him.

"If I see another pretty sunset, I'll ask the captain to eject dirty engine oil all over, killing all the fish, rare whales, and other creatures."

A day passes. Yellow walls pull in the early morning sunlight through the blinds. Layers of ice on the black driveway melt, causing massive floods in developing countries. Throughout the fast spring, dimensionless robins, loaded with undefeatable viruses, sing in the pine trees, making my attempt at getting any sleep nearly impossible. I'm sitting in a red leather chair watching the river flow outside. I've been looking at a picture book about zoos—photographs of shiny black panthers in cages. I put the book aside and pick up the Koran. As I turn a page, an oval-shaped patch of light settles on a passage. Who remembers dreams after seventy-five years of age?

Anver is fatigued and his face is well beyond the skills of even the best face-lifter surgeon to make young again. A happiness hovers around his eyes; he inhales the air in front of him and exhales a story with faulty linkages because his memory is not as vast as mine. This is not a consequence of old age, nor a consequence of class. We went to Lahore together and to Sussex and to Oman, and to see the Marsh Arabs, and to Jordan to see the King but he wouldn't see us, so we made friends with locals. We met a Hafez El Assad Syrian lookalike, whose name could have been Dmitri or something like that and who gave us tea and biscuits. Anver reminds me that we never went to Dagestan. Dmitri told us not to go because he said South Asian Englishmen like us were far too broad-minded, that we spoke English far too well, that we knew how to eat properly with forks and knives, and we shouldn't talk to people with names like Dzhanet Magomedov or Umalat Abdullayeva. I told him we weren't exactly South Asian Englishmen.

Anver shifts in his chair and, with his prattle, has now taken me, in thought, somewhere we were. I'm again on the deck of the ship that is crossing the Atlantic. We had to cross the Atlantic after the flash and bang in London. It's a coincidence we ended up in the same old folks home. He smiles and walks down the hall to his room.

During some months at our old folks home, he does not show up for lunch, or for dinner, or for breakfast the following day, but today we're sitting together again at the end of a hallway, the windows giving out to a view of the river outside. It's the afternoon and, somehow, another twilight approaches as we cross the Atlantic during a day in a month in the current calendar. We did sometimes use the other calendar, but the numbers were always lower; in fact everything was lower.

Portside, a gull glides along with us on the moving ship. It sheers back out to the sea, does a stall turn, and is back beside the ship. It nicks the window and flies off, unhurt. Anver observes: "Gull. Beak. Blood. Death." The seeds of a lifelong operational friendship are sown at forty-five degrees latitude and the same longitude, just down the street from another ship. I just hope no one comes to interview him.

As planned, two days after the event, we left the U.K. on this passenger ship from Southampton. The authorities caught the wrong people and then, these authorities—who when you get right down to it are all patrician idiots—flashed brown faces all over the newspapers.

I have difficulty sleeping on water. Anver suggests that I focus my eyes on one star. This will help me sleep. I turn down the well-lit corridor whose windows give out on to the sea. I go to my room and look out of my window and stare at a star outside.

Although the ship is cutting the sea, I hear the trickling of a canal somewhere underneath me. Canal and ocean in the same place? How can I hear a canal with all this sea and wind around me? Is it not the old water table that is drying out under the old folks home? With the dry summers in Pierrefonds, the clay on which the home is built is contracting because the tarmac on the roads prevents rain water from maintaining the density of the clay. The home, like the ship I was on, is moving, slithering on soft clay, propellers slowly churning through it, moving it forward in small increments. I see a spot of sunlight on a bottle of wine, and then I see the bearded man in a painting by Manet. Or is it a photograph by Cartier-Bresson, 1938—what's it called? "Au bords de la Marne"? Perhaps it is "Le déjeuner sur l'herbe," 1863. One of the kids looks like the young Malcolm X. I read art history with a minor in bomb making at a university east of Cardiff or Toronto, I forget.

Within a canvas someone trickles wine into a glass. The trickling sounds like the canals in Amsterdam, where we did lots of work to make Dutch society truly liberal. In the canvas, they're having a picnic: table cloth, French culture, cheese, long rowboat with a pointy bow in the background. The man in the painting has a wife who is beautiful by the standards of the period. She is black, not white as in the original painting. Mulatto kids play in the sunshine with a Sikh boy who has a kirpan attached to his belt and looks like a kid in Kabul. The white kids keep their distance. This painting of the middle classes, once populated by white Europeans, now has various sized Malcolm X figurines standing in the same places, eating paan and samosas and drinking lassi.

The painted characters run out of their frozen positions, play on the river bank and then return to their previous postures. The lips and mouths in the canvas open. The wife in the image says: "Passe-moi le something,

something," as the surface flutters in the fresh sea air. The bearded man replies: "Voilà." Everyone makes rustling noises when they move because they are speaking and moving in canvas. Bones poke through the painting. Painted flesh and clothing make the image bulge like a wave. Particles fall off the painting. The European canvas rises upwards revealing a foaming sea.

Days and nights pass. I smell land, but there isn't land anywhere. Anver used to stand on the highest deck to look for land. Now, I'm looking for Canada. What am I looking at—the sea behind a see-through canvas? White grammar school kids have appeared in the canvas. They are dressed in school uniforms and make tick-tock sounds as they shift through the scene. They too have small kirpans attached to their sides.

At noon, the day before our arrival, I look down into the moving water. Is it possible that I can see the Russell Square tube stop under the Atlantic? Just my imagination—must be. When the tube doors open, passengers with lead shoes walk the ocean floor among the telegraph cables from the last century, attending to a service in an underwater mosque. The passengers put their ears to the barnacle-covered steel and hear the conversations between Eisenhower and Tony Blair, trapped in cable memory which has a low decay rate. I hear rustling sounds behind me. The shoo-shoo of the deciduous leaves in wind and the sea waves mix. Bits of the altered European paintings return to my mind. Picasso's "Les Demoiselles d'Avignon" changes into women wearing tight blue jeans made by a fashion company that stitches their brand name in gold letters on the back—*Hejaz Jeans*, their finger nails painted flesh silver pink, holding cubist chickens in their hands. The mummified canvas breaks up. Snowy particles now fall over the North Atlantic; these European models, once living things, are wrapped in a thin gauze.

We're approaching the coast. I hear the seagulls in the distance. Am I carrying guilt with me? Generally, guilt is an influential interpretation of interpretation. The land smells confirm that we've been smart enough not to leave a trail for the British authorities: we're safely on a luxury ship which has almost crossed. A few hours later, the land approaches us; chain links, heavy as elephants, moor us to the Canadian land mass. We walk down the steps into a harbour.

We were young and had to pull Canada from her deep slumber. And now, we're old. At breakfast in the home, Anver asks me if I know what Benzene Pars is? Farsi for British Petroleum I tell him.

At conception, within my Moslem mother, was I destined to be a mole? A mole all my life or just part of it, and which part—the front or the back part? Terrorism and cellular reality—inseparable. Anver and the others who were from various cellular backgrounds had been given an understanding of Islam, and I helped them to understand a white fist in the face. I use the word *various*: he doesn't. The mullah at a mosque in a topical part of London also helped Anver to understand things as they are. This mullah was such a liberal that he had a Cornish pig as a pet, a pet he would bring to the mosque on Fridays. With his new enlightenment, Anver would assert views like: Integrated middle-class Moslems can't appreciate the extent to which we have been screwed by the West. This is why Iran has to test a nuke. They don't need a nuke, they have the Strait of Hormouz, I used to reply. He didn't have the knowledge to go much beyond this level of reasoning. We didn't require more reasoning. He himself suspected that his class origins were behind the fact that he didn't have and couldn't develop a deeper understanding, but this only made him a better team player. And, there were others like him. Others came and went—none *went* in the media sense. He's here with me today, not in paradise or Nymphenberger petting the drum-tight hymens of virgins.

I've thought about how he grew up. He had training in chemistry, physics, and West Yorkshire English. His father ran a garage which serviced a few Islamic cars and where, as a young man, Anver worked part-time. His father sent him to good schools where science was taken seriously and encouraged him to distance himself from friends with green cars. Anver understood the modernism in his father but liked, or should I say loved, to work at the local level, and far from his father's control. We took many trips in small lorries to London and to small towns near the western tip of England, and parked overnight. Then, at some point, we decided the lorries would flash apart with a fifty-two minute delay between bangs. But they were modest bangs—even Anver's integrated father said that they were very modest. We bombed a part of little England. Any rational, left-voting English Moslem could see that exploitation was increasing. We knew this small non-event counted only for practice. The ruling classes had to hire more journalists to cover the flash and smoke. These humble events we conducted pulled in the larger funders. And then things got far, far from conventional. This required us to imagine things we never thought of. We conducted events vaster than the liberation armies of Northern Ireland, Spain et cetera el Europa.

Where am I now?

In the old folks home?

Or am I a young man in London doing another set of events?

Did I see the paintings in my mother's womb? Will I mastermind events in Canada's nice cities? What were the icebergs if not amniotic fluid in another form? And why did they all lean in the same direction? What force pulled them? What force pulled me down along my mother's canal? That we immigrated, or were vectored here or were born here, makes no difference; makes all the difference. Do we care if we get caught? We'll progress even if they catch us. Societies transform when we're in their prisons. Do we get tortured in various cities in the dark world? We don't have much to tell because we're not an organized army. In their prisons, we become Islamic gold. They can't say that they've finished with us; we're right there in their prisons. And we have family and friends who make life worth living.

The Canadian coast awakens me. What was I in England? Who am I now? What have I become? How many airports did I move through? Why is the concept of forgiveness as strange as acquiring Lunar citizenship? Is it impossible for us to forget cotton becoming shirts? Am I the man in the airport waiting for the flight to equality?

I look at our ship's black hull as we drive away. Anver Ahmed born in Sialkot, near Bradford cosmologically speaking. We ate fish and chips, ate Paya on Fridays, ate Baysin-ke-roti, and knew how to re-calibrate camshafts —top dead centre, bottom dead centre. He joined us in international stuff from Anchorage to Ulan Bator. We regretted doing Ulan but, somehow, we just had to wake them from a dun landscape that allows for centuries of slumber.

2

Chanel Vegas Collection

The first sign that things have changed is when you can't hear anything. You're under a large, protective dome that's hovering metres above your head.

Then the lecture hall has an odour coming from Noam not because he's old but because of the melting glass. The lights in the hall flicker and manufactured things become, as you used to say, de-manufactured. If you're wearing glasses, shadowy and clear bars like an interference pattern form on your lenses. The seconds feel like hours. Sound and vision entangle at a level we studied at school.

Before the smoke, a silent white flash fills the halls: Buddhism meets Islam as you said once or twice. Noam's words can't be heard. The protective sound dome saves us from his words. Seconds ago, he said: "The slaughter in East Timooo ..." The lights flicker like thin clouds moving across a full moon over the Bay of Fundy. I can see you laughing because I just mentioned a place in Canada? If you're *in* all that fire, the damage happens slowly: an airborne pen travels through a hat, and then through the face of an undergraduate; his eyes and nose are now an oval flesh and blood mix that hovers in space before streaking into the wall. An iPad spins itself into a Frisbee which snaps a neck then fractures into parts of eyes and lips, app icons, so on and so forth. No matter how slow these events seem to the victims, to an amused, distant, viewer like Anver, events move fast. In the blink of an eye, everything except large structures revert to dust.

Joseph, you think I'll tell the cops what we did. I won't do anything of the sort, but, Joseph, I think I should tell you that I'll die today. I know you're going to find this letter because I put it in one of the books you're reading.

I know you're here to make sure we don't tell anyone. Why would you think this? I know you'll find this note, and when you read it, it'll be like hearing my voice say your name. We're almost the same age and we're both mentally sound. I also made notes all the time, just like you. I've had a meaningful life with you, working side by side; nothing spoilt our connection. You're the loveliest. What were the chances I'd be working with you? We didn't get caught because our advisors used some kind of higher thinking to decrease the chances of getting caught when the cards were stacked against us. What does stacked mean? Does it mean that things are predetermined?

On my way to this operation, I ran into my neighbour on the way to pick you up. Was this a case of predetermination? No, not really, but I think about it all the time. Why wouldn't I? This was my operation. On this particular bombing you were just another follower. About five hundred were to get killed. Lofty? Yes, but nothing happens if you don't set goals.

In preparation for those fall term blasts, I remember filing my nails and slowly, pushing the half-moons into the light of a warm-tone light bulb, putting on gold nail polish. I know you like looking at my dark complexion with gold. Lunch is set at such and such a time and place, after which, a bomb will explode at a large lecture hall where he'll be speaking in front of hundreds of students: and, thank Allah, in front of the public at large. See how useful Chanel Vegas Collection, Le Vernis Gold Fingers Nail Polish can be? Nothing like Vegas to distract us Moslems from the killings.

Daylight enters from the floor-to-ceiling windows that surround the lecture hall. Tree leaves sway outside. Room lights, spectacles, ceramic glass on phones break into millions of bits, due to the radically new stuff we're using. It takes about two hundred hours and/or three centuries for the dust to really settle.

Someone in our group did the calculations for the job. And, of course, we calculated the radius islamicus, which was many, many metres. Bathetically, an innocent wall crumbles onto running students and the public at large. Thank Allah. Why did all of us in this group of terrorists study science? Their terrorism against us is so strong because their science is stronger than ours. So we connected science plus morals plus innocent intestines flowing up walls.

Joseph, I'm thinking about our past: wet sound waves hit the ears like an insulting slap from a Mullah in Yorkshire. Upper-middle class students listen to inoffensive words by Noam; he tells them a story of how Arafat told him that the hippocampus is the most anti-terrorist part of the brain so we should have moved Israelis to a hippocampus near Camden.

Some of the things you used to say made me laugh.

Things made of glass are coming to an end and, in fact, life itself is coming to an end. Sheets of smoke, shoes, arms, legs, throats, and detached fingers and toes zip past. Bits of flesh stretch out like billowing large, pink tents, then deflate like old balloons; bodies flying overhead, roll on their own axes and hit the walls.

And why haven't we been hit? Well, because you and I are in the MRI room getting treated for terrorism. The MRI room is near where we are doing today's bang.

Joseph, it's because of you, and practising with you, that I've been near enough to smaller test explosions to feel the initial hot silence. The white flash means paradise for the engulfed ones: just compensation for having known The Faerie Queene better than the works of Mohammad for all those years.

Joseph, I knew how to think clearly before I met you, but I could never do what I'm doing today were it not for you and only you who encouraged women to conceive, plan and execute bombings even when menstruating, jam rags expanding to infinity and back.

We did another bombing before our main bombing. Why am I telling you when you already know? I am reminding you for the pleasure of reminding you. An Israeli politician was invited by a local political party to visit them at their office; we did lightweight cultural bangs. From our point of view these were non-terrorist bombings, no matter how the city interpreted them. The city aquarium, we read in the papers, had three small bull sharks. When our tiny bombs shattered the glass several people were injured by sharks flapping around on the flooded floor. Two kids, one Moslem we learned later, were bitten, one lost a leg, and their bonsai collection accidentally caught fire, which we regretted. Most Moslems I know respect bonsai trees as much as they respect religion. We did small damage: one leg and a few bites, far from balancing things. Of course, nothing to fill us with guilt or anything like that. As well, we bombed the Côte-Saint-Luc metro station at 3:30 in the morning. 'Twas only coincidence no one got killed. We spread these events across several hours just to ratchet up the tension. You agreed with me about bombing the fish before getting the international talent speaking at McGill. Surf and turf on the menu for today. And, in a strange way we can see it as liberating fish from zoos. We couldn't get the animal liberation people to support us even though our struggles were similar. Saving a whale is much like saving a Moslem. You used to say that some whales have converted to Islam and from the deep, cold Atlantic, they send sound-messages to Haram al-Sharif.

After lunch, we had to go to the hospital as cover. I remember making you hold my hand in the car on the way to the hospital. I don't like going to the hospital at all, but we have to go because of the funding. Nothing to do with health, or perhaps a bit to do with health. I must be mentally ill or I'm a pretend-patient with normal looking appointments in an excellent research hospital getting MRIs or CT scans simply to have a cover.

In the car on the way to the hospital, your hand enveloped mine and I felt gushy, as we headed south on Avenue du Parc and turned right on Pine, autumn leaves flapping ostentatiously on both sides. We turn right into the underground parking at the Royal Victoria Hospital.

We arrive to get the final technical assistance for the five-hundred-people-job we're doing today. But, I am still being tested for something; I mean I have something which has to be confirmed or not confirmed. So two, rather than three, birds with one stone: I get my scan; we get more funding from our connection.

As we enter the grey building with carved wooden doorways, I remember you turning your head south to take a look at the skyscrapers in downtown Montreal, the Saint Lawrence river in the far distance, the university —nursery of Canadian imperialism—nestled in the foreground. You looked in the direction of the lecture hall and looked at me. The metal-skinned elevator takes us to the fourth floor. In the waiting room, under the fluorescent lights, you sit down to read a magazine from the last century. Holding a pad, the nurse, with a Jamaican accent, asks for me. Usha. I'm Irish but nicknamed Usha —you thought that up.

I leave you holding a copy of *Time Magazine* with an old British prime minister, Harold Macmillan, on the cover. I get up, smiling, and follow the nurse to the MRI theatre, where I slide into a blue frock. My toes and the arch of my feet that you love touching settle on the cold floor. I've been here a few times. Funding plus supplies for bombs and coordination always take a few visits to the Neuro. The nurse knows me. I like her. I've been coming here twice a year for years, I lie down on a long steel tray and the god of blinking pin lights and small beeps pulls me into the plastic cylinder which could, with the right quantity of C4, launch me across the park and into upper Westmount among the wood pigeons. What might I see on such a flight? Trees with bright fall colours, above me the stars receding. Whose roof would I fall through? What would the rich families be talking about at dinner time? I ask the nurse if she could launch me into outer space. I tell her that I could accelerate the effects of the circus explosive by pushing with all the thunder in my thighs. If I'm in low orbit my friends will not have to worry about me. Oh, she's doing orbital terrorism now—using lasers to bomb satellites—don't worry about her. But here, Joseph, in the *duniya* of the small, provincial world of electrons I am stationary. I'll live in this cylinder for the next forty-five minutes. What will they see inside me? I suspect I have something.

All the health bills are paid by our terrorist stock exchange, all set up by a Moslem with a shaved snatch. *Allah o akbar* to the razors meeting flesh not far from the clit, just the hair, not the clit. You'd pretend to be Max Planck as you touched my clit. Oh Max, oh Max, I can't believe you gave me a hand job in Yad Vashem after you trimmed my hairs with a razor—your trained hand removing the hair so the clit could stick its head out and dare that Islamic edge.

These men and women of the MRI machines must conduct mission after deep mission into my body. While I'm here, I think, what's Joseph doing now, is he still reading that *Time Magazine* or has he picked up one of the old *National Geographics* I saw stacked on a coffee table in the waiting room? The MRI room has a high ceiling and fluorescent lights. Later, you're in my MRI room, sitting in the chair in the corner, faint, yellow-coloured walls rising behind you. It looks like we're in an old folks home but we aren't; we're here at a research hospital.

Why do I have to go through the MRI every time? Cover. I just do as you ask. You see me lying on the tray, slowly sliding into the plastic world. I smile slightly and move my legs.

I teach high school part-time, grades seven and eight. I'm tired. I've adjusted my makeup for the second, third, and fourth time today, red lips, fine black outlines for my eyes. I'm a bunch of nerves. All day. Nerves, but calm nerves. The tube envelops me like a placenta in rigor mortis. Strangely, the buzzing and knocking sounds cause me to daydream, but not sleep. The nurse won't allow me to doze.

The sounds of science comfort me; they become chimes on a porch in a Montreal suburb. The liquid they inject into my arm heats me. I feel the heat every time. Are they giving me a CT Scan or an MRI? Here, Joseph, is what I saw in my daydream while I was in the scan tube: I'm at a terrorist meeting in Toronto where a young woman is telling me about how she met her husband at a test bombing in Sudan. Civilized people go to openings for Jeff Koons, we go to test bombings. She keeps talking: Islam this and Islam that. We have a similar educational background but her chatter is making my head hurt and I can't escape her empty religious talk. I keep thinking about Jeff Koons' colourful bunnies. We approached this artist to make a fifty metre shiny abstract version of Mohammad (PBUH) receiving revelations.

In the corner of the large room, you and someone that looks like Anver—perhaps a doctor—are talking.

There isn't a nurse here. She's behind glass, away from the electrons.

The man with a black beard says hello. You both go into a smaller room leaving me in the plastic cylinder which is making buzzing sounds like house-trance music made by a hipster from Cologne, and for a moment I feel guilty that I'll be playing a key part in blowing up *such* a prestigious person. Why I've agreed to do this I don't know. We're not going to blow it up now—not right this very minute. I'm here getting tested and treated for terrorism, so we have a few minutes before things go splat, loud noise, and an awful lot of smoke. And we can't stop the bomb now. What if at the last minute the university changes the location of the lecture?

Why would a doctor help us destroy lives here in Montreal? All this killing of people sometimes baffles me, but I go on doing it. I guess it's nothing but retaliation, or defense, or just a job like working at a shoe store or teaching at a university. Today, I am on my period so of course I'm having doubts about blowing up students, and the public at large. Yes, I blame self-doubt on my period. I'll take some more Islamic Midol—it expired in 632 AD but I'll take my chances. The Great Book does not forbid women to bomb when bleeding. Joseph, my love I'm saying all this to make you laugh. We won't tell the cops and we won't tell the mullahs we called you the Red Leader.

Then, suddenly, the tray on which I've been lying starts to move. My exam is over and the nurse says that if there is anything Dr. Changberg will call me. They always say there's nothing new. "New" is a question of degree. I live my life, the electrons, theirs.

A few minutes from now, when the famous thinker speaks, everything will change. From our point of view, they'll have to scrape off the flesh and rebuild that particular wing of the university. Perhaps they will do this with Saudi money. McGill gets new wings built with Saudi money. Directly, or indirectly: did Wahabi cosmology fund us also? Do you remember or is your brain going also? Does it matter who funds this? It's all Allah's funding in the end, the good and the bad.

While getting funding for the very next thing, we cause the worst collective haemorrhage in Canadian university history, but they made weapons and sold them to the wrong types. Can we justify what we did? Perhaps only to ourselves. About today: I swear I felt the bomb blast right here in this medical instrument. The nurse tells me that something has happened. What? I ask. People are running out of the building, I can see and hear ambulances. Within hours, downtown Montreal will be in Kandaharian lockdown, just like we caused in, as you used to say, Marlowe's London.

With finesse, I slip off the blue frock and look at my tits and wonder if the MRI has jostled my tit-mind continuum: after a CT scan or MRI I never know if my tits are in the same time zone. You and I both have advanced degrees in terror related science and engineering, and I have the largest breasts of any woman terrorist in the world. Lots of women did lots of killing. The press showed nothing, just the extremists beating women, which, in a way, was far from the truth.

I put on my not-so-high heels and walk over to pick you up in the waiting room. I don't walk quickly. The nurse and a guard tell us to head home right away. Someone in the waiting room says it was bomb. We act shocked, but not unhappy. Pretending to be unhappy would make us hypocrites, which is forbidden, just like having the red sea flowing down your legs during these events. Aden to Port Said, then across to Yad Vashem for a red squirt orgasm on all the saddening photos.

We meet back in the waiting room. You've heard the news. You smile as I pull you from an old *National Geographic* featuring *Eisenhower's* visit to a large country which has lots of mosques. Joseph, why did Ike visit Pakistan? We take *Eisenhower to your apartment with us as a memento, when we arrive* you do it to me on the corner of the bed. You ask me to say: *I love killing people, especially the innocent ones who are out for a day of shopping while the other half ... et cetera blah blah.* I do as you say, etc. etc., etc. Joseph, I always do as you say. You blow your load into my red *paratha* and I cover my lack of having an orgasm, at least the sex made me laugh. As usual, I almost come. I think laughing is more important than the hidden Imam who is coming. I'm sort of bleeding just like all the students at McGill did a few hours ago. You came quickly, because of Ramadan. I wondered if we were actually in Ramadan. Perhaps a good laugh is better than an orgasm? You put your head down on the pillow and become my adorable friend.

I see lightning from your sparse nineteenth floor apartment window at Sherbrooke and Saint Denis. Your apartment has Ikea tables, chair, this bed we're on, the book shelves, and on top of the glass Expedit bookshelf on wheels, a do-it-yourself Ikea super-small kiloton nuclear bomb. You're on the bed. I ask: "Where's that from?"

In a clear voice from the polka-dotted black and white Ikea pillow you reply: "From Mohammad's Neurological Inconsistency."

From your balcony we see the city covered with heavy rain, ambulances and police cars moving in the streets. No sirens, just flashing police car lights. We come back into the bedroom. A coma, like the near-coma I experienced in the scan tube, now engulfs us. We sleep soundly for about an hour, and then slowly, we pull out of the cone of sleep, get up and drive to Jean Talon, an area which we'll never bomb. Hindu *dosas* arrive at our table, conversation seems unnecessary. We've had rather a good day. On the way back to the car, we laugh at the wet streets reflecting upside down neon Urdu.

Now, I am super old. You live down the hall from me. You watch me day and night. I can't believe we drenched all those innocents in their own blood and the blood of others while I myself was having a heavy flow day. See how I've been influenced by your sense of humour?

We've come to this home to die, but they've made it so hard to die. You come to sleep with me sometimes. One just goes on living. It's the medicines they give us. We simply can't die. It's terrorism to keep us alive. The sun rises, we wake. We're still alive. We can't undo medical advances and they can't undo their state terrorism. The medical advances keep us fit for more work. Maybe we'll get younger and start all over again but this time with larger bombs. The big powers are still winning, there's work to be done. We don't want to live, yet they make us live. We are bored, endlessly bored with simple things such as breathing and eating.

Joseph, you're the coldest: the murders don't come back to you. You always murdered in a forward sense. You don't want anyone to confess our lovely bombings to the press. Journalists have come by, but that could be Anver playing the fool, at your instigation, testing our faculties against a clock that spins as fast as a Frisbee on a summer day, a winter's day, a spring day.

Our potential leakage keeps your memory from failing. You also take pills for memory improvement. You think one of us will leak? All this keeps you young.

You tell me these days, old people are more energetic than old folks in the past. You want us to have ordinary ends, but how can we have ordinary ends when we're exceptional people who've never been caught?

The McGill job was not as good as we'd hoped. Only 295 killed, and some will have to spend the rest of their lives in wheelchairs. These numbers will not put us on the honour list. *Inshallah*, we'll improve. To put things coarsely, Noam became vapour by explosives researched and developed by blah blah blah MITs all over the world, but alas, I repeat myself.

Some of the field terrorists working on this bombing make lunches for their kids. A friend who helped us had to go home to make dinner for her kids, and they were going to watch Seinfeld and other Jewish comedy programmes such as the Big Terrorist Crunch.

You, Joseph were and are fuelled by something larger, I don't know what that was, maybe that's why you kept dreaming up bigger and bigger ways to balance things. *Inshallah*, I'll die now. Forgive me for leaving—I mean dying. You made me laugh insanely. Joseph, these will be my last words, so much for their monopoly on violence.

3

Lahore, Atlantic, LHR

Not only did Dr. Rosa Luxemberg wear a tight-fitting blue suit with a fuchsia blouse that boldly revealed what Islam might reshape with hydrochloric acid, she also had an *I-will-not-look-away-from-your-eyes-because-I-am-in-the-Islamic World* confidence flowing through her.

A day ago, she flew in from Austin, Texas, and today, during a sunny Friday afternoon, she went to visit Joseph at his office on the university campus. Her shoulder-length wavy blonde hair helped her personable smile when she spoke with Joseph. He was tall, fine-featured, had a light complexion, and had understated, consequential leadership abilities.

Luxemberg offered Joseph a job at her university in Austin, not only because he was a promising mathematician, but because he was also someone who, as a young man, knew about things in other distant fields: Elitzur-Vaidman testing problems and string theory, to mention two. With his travel paper work complete, his contract signed, and with a view to living permanently in America, he went to Allama Iqbal Airport and left the ancient city.

Although Joseph was not in any way connected to cricket, he made it a habit to frequently telephone the members of the campus cricket team, and he went to on- and off-campus meetings with the Lahore Abroad Cricket Team. There were not altogether surprising consequences to his many phone calls and meetings with other members of LACT. These meetings did not interfere with his work as a mathematician, but after the presentation of his much-awaited paper, he felt he should leave America, where he had lived for about five years.

Day 1, Flight 035, 24 Dhu l-Hijja AH 1408

Ten thousand metres below him, the Atlantic slips by, and within hours the Texas afternoon changes to a starry night. A few hours later, as they move toward Heathrow, a thin band of red sunlight peels the dark blue horizon: the plane is nearing Ireland, and then over historic Lockerbie with its Libyan restaurants offering Maghreban complexities in the stomach of a goat. Our *sable earth, mother of dread and fear,* gently curves. The descent to Heathrow has begun. A newer life will begin. Hissing engines move the passengers over the troubles, a layer of skin growing over their orange eyes.

Earlier, before the flight, at the ticket counter at George Bush International Airport, Joseph noticed two tall, pot-bellied men in ten-gallon hats wander around the boarding gates; then two beefy Immigration and Naturalization Service officials: one, a black man, dressed in a white T-shirt and black jeans, placed his hand on the check-in counter at Houston Airport. The shades of black between the inside of his palm and the back of his hand is distinct enough to make a clear line from pink to black. Joseph remembers staring at these hands for what seemed like five minutes.

As the plane banks, sunlight scrapes the inside walls of the cabin. Coffee laced with caustic soda is served by a flight attendant with blonde eyes *and* blonde hair and a steel helmet with horns.

Two Arabs, sitting a few seats to the side, move constantly in their seats. They are planning something. They're dressed in expensive suits, but they don't wear ties. "Flying 747s for Dummies" falls out of the seat pouch. They get up. The passengers, in unison, bury their eyes into their newspapers only to peek over the top edges. Everyone watches them. The Saudis return from the toilet singing a version of "Okie from Muskogee." What kind of notes did they leave in the washroom? Joseph imagines he will see the following written on a napkin in the washroom:

> *I see water and God. Allah and pure water —some salt in water. Now. Ready for final Atlantic landing, please to inform Allah of my virtuees in earthely life. There Is No God but Allahs and Mohammad (PBUH) is the last pilot of Islam—not in plural—singularly only. Pray now. We will not land. We see for the last time. Excuse to my english. It is write by arab man who is god servant. In the name of God, the compassionate, the Mercifful ...*
>
> *Yours truly,*
> *Wa-sabi'*

There is no flight attendant with an open jugular vein squirting blood onto the cabin windows. There isn't a broken vodka bottle on the floor. The seat belts alert lights flash. Are they planning new ways to paralyze the western world? Are they going to put something in the water supply that will make all of Philadelphia deaf as a pomegranate from Kandahar? Will they inject zeros and ones into national TV that will show the president making a speech in Pashto? One of the Arabs calls for water. A camel with blue eyes and a southern drawl pulls water out of the well in the flying oasis.

The Americans weren't comfortable with their faces: otherwise there wasn't a problem. Drinking water and pissing it out is not the work of non-state actors.

While listening to Brahms, Joseph gets up to go the washroom. He found the CD somewhere in the airport. Maybe he should not go through with this. Maybe he should go back to this:

$$F = MA$$

$$\text{Fazil} = \text{Mohammad} \bullet \text{Anver}$$

Or perhaps he should return to something he saw in his alphabet soup:

$$E = hf$$

$$\text{Eram} = \text{Hafeez} \bullet \text{Fazil}$$

He thinks about getting rid of all his identity cards in the toilet.

The plastic covered photos are difficult to snap. The airline ticket receipt is shredded easily. A National Bank of America credit card refuses to bend and break. He drops it into the toilet bowl intact and uses his hand to push it through the vortex, while drops of the blue water climb up to his wrist. His finger touches the spot where the exhausted airplane food of thousands has passed. A travel document with a long serial number flows over Saint Mungo Street, Glasgow. The ink-stamped words "temporary" and "cancelled" are visible on the pages of a removal document. A photo of his face sticks to the grey metal toilet bowl. In a toilet at 8000 metres and falling, Joseph stares at photogenic Joseph looking as earnest as Gandhi standing in a corn field in Punjab, tube in hand, giving himself a Hindu identity enema. The blue water, flowing in a tight blue spiral, ripples over his face. The suction flush obliterates *Brahms* and *Gandhi*. Every bit of proof is scattered over the mutinous waves near Helensburgh. The proof of who he is spreads all over Scotland. As he returns to his seat, his papers still in order, he hears:

> *It is now 7:05 local time and the temperature on the ground is 15 degrees Celsius. As you can see, we have scattered clouds and light showers. As your captain, I apologize for the delay at Houston but I hope your flight has been enjoyable. Have a good stay in London and thank you for flying with us.*

The passengers shift through the elephant trunk into transit. Everyone seems to be going where they need to be, but he's lost. He walks a little faster. No baggage claim to worry about. He must get rid of his olive suit and white polyester shirt. He must change his clothes. Can any security people identify him? Anything left behind in a pocket or in the suitcase? There is a small rip on the left shoulder—maybe they'll remember this? His hair flops neatly over his ears. He turns into a corridor and disappears into the crowd. Fatigue sets in as he tries to recover from the flight. A voice spreads in transit: "Please do not leave your luggage unattended. All unattended luggage will be seized and searched. Ne laissez pas vos baggages ..." In German, Spanish, Arabic, and others.

As he falls asleep, the languages become a hive of sounds. A turmeric-coloured fog drips from the bodies of the parked aircraft. Dark nose-cones poke through the vapour which, cyclically speaking, was produced by all the burning jet fuel. A black private jet, its undercarriage obscured in fog, floats into a hangar.

Will the fog cover LHR for a century? Men in orange overalls moor the last of the antique jumbos; by their movements, the jumbos, nod back to the men. A flock of Tibetan monks wearing long saffron gowns float into transit. Passengers crowd the waiting rooms and toilets. Heathrow is inefficient. The toilet line-ups are long. The toilet floors are now watery due to the volume of traffic. This disgusts the Europeans; the Asians, especially the South Asians, are more understanding, walking on tippy toes through a shallow field of diluted urine.

People are sleeping, sitting, reading books and newspapers; they wait for the fog to lift, or for their turn at the toilet. On a long grey bench, a man snores. A nun tries to read but is distracted by the snoring. Daniel in the den with lions. In the far distance, Joseph with his trolley strolls through the immobilized crowd. He's the only one moving. A closed umbrella swings like a fruit bat from his trolley. He walks out of the toilet wearing a Brazilian national team football jersey. His briefcase rests on the trolley. He moves through terminal F, past gate 12, past the Air India counter. He walks to a rubber plant near the farthest wall of the terminal, then back to the Icelandair departure gate, which is packed with passengers. He stares at the flickering flight announcement board: Jordanian Airlines 0973, via Vienna to Calcutta—delayed. Strangely, this disappoints him; he sits on a bench and looks around. He notices two identical pot-bellied Sikh men in their forties. They're wearing identical yellow turbans and pink starched shirts. They are motionless, asleep, turbans touching. Joseph removes his earphones, sits down in front of the snoring twins and closes his eyes and falls asleep. The announcement board flutters like a flock of birds lifting into the air: BA Copenhagen ON TIME: FLT: 047: boarding. The wait could take days. How long will he remain undetected? Why am I waiting in an airport? Why the uncertainty in principle? Are they watching? Is waiting in the airport for so many days a professional way to conduct terrorism?

The fog defeats the powerful airport lights, small matchsticks in a forest at night. What was here before the airplanes? A pre-toxic meadow with cows? Peasants resisting aristocratic land encroachments? Centuries hiss by. A hand touches his shoulders. A sari-clad Air India attendant with a red spot the size of a one pound coin on her forehead in clear Glaswegian asks: "Sorry to wake you up sir, but aren't you waiting for the Calcutta flight?" Joseph stares at the departure gate. Everyone has boarded. The sun is shining outside. "Huh?" he musters. Leaning towards him, the attendant waits for an answer. He doesn't look at her directly but at the ceiling-mounted security camera. A moving walkway transports him and his trolley to terminal G and the routine of the wait in transit. He sleeps.

Day 2, 25 Dhul Hijjah 1408

From high above at sunset, the airport must look like an insect with long legs. Glowing, red-orange roads snake out from its concrete shell like veins in a bloodshot eye. Inside, Heathrow comes back to life. Shiny aircraft move along the tarmac, runway markers, C-47, C-46 are blocked from view, then reappear as the aircraft moves. The tail fin of an SAS plane cuts through the sunlight that falls on Joseph's face.

He walks away from the Sikhs, and then a few minutes later he returns to sit in front of the two yellow-turbaned men who are still touching each other's dreams. The static swirls of their turbans resemble the rotation of the fan blades of a parked 747. Perhaps, he daydreams, the slowly turning blades will undo their turbans, pulling their long hair into the turbines.

Sikhs dream about nothing but food. One of the

sleeping Sikhs must be dreaming about *aloo parathas*. A paratha slowly floats up out of his turban into the humming air of transit and floats down into the other Sikh's turban-mind. Transit passengers stop and observe the mind transfer. Joseph spreads out on a bench and pulls his coat over his head. Two security guards walk past him. Under the safety of his coat, he imagines a black and white security monitor in the airport secure zone revealing him sleeping on a bench next to a tall living palm tree, sleeping as thirty million passengers pass by his nose.

The PA system calls for a lost Mr. Fazool Samundur, or Ms. Lal Chout, or a Mrs. Penny Point to come to the information desk. Perhaps when his partners arrive he'll hear a silky cathedral voice stating throughout transit: "Your fellow terrorists have arrived—they're all dressed in black."

There is a large TV screen in Bon Voyage, a local transit café. Peela Dakhavaa is on strike, and team captain Imran Zindagee Ultaa has set an attacking field, with two short legs, a silly point, and a man out on the pull at deep third man. Is the television sending him a message?

A school of irrational sadhus wearing saffron robes, surrounded by ancient mists, walk by the Singapore Airlines gate. They've arrived in England via fifteen hours of rational means. Inside their bags-with-sandalwood-handles lie musical instruments, small black lacquered boxes, incense, and bifocals. Tanned shoulders. Buddhist passports are never dog-eared. Their periodic presence here always brings the sensation that the air within transit is renewing itself. But it isn't. There isn't any wind, except when a whirring airport cart comes by driven by a red-nosed driver with a plastic ID dangling from his neck. There aren't any fluctuations in temperature, even the sunshine, which scrapes across in window-like forms, can't alter it. From Bon Voyage, he can see a monk purchasing a Braun electric shaver.

Surrounded by glass, he can't hear the geriatric jumbos landing on the tarmac, plumes of burning rubber in long, white screeches. 19:05 — a creaking Ilyushin grumbles off to Moscow. Nearby, a jumbo taxies to a predetermined gate, wings drooping from Bengali fatigue. Dhaka enters, causing him to think of Mohammad Anver and Mohammad Iqbal. When will they arrive?

A pinpoint of light in the evening sky — this could be them — slowly becomes a vast Airbus bringing lung infections, the first cases of Variant Creutzfeldt-Jakob disease, contraband, and illegals who provide jobs for lawyers.

On Bon Voyage's wall-mounted TV, two of the obedient moons, Io and Europa, orbit through odourless transit, penned in by glass and stainless steel. Europa hovers through security cameras concealed in upside-down opaque bowls that look like the eyes of a dead cat. Joseph gets dizzy looking around at the world that Lord Heathrow, from the grave, makes.

The black, green, and red tail fin of an Arab airline brings three barrel-bodied Moslem clerics. Gulls and cormorants with night vision look for food outside among the heaps of steel; one flaps its wings into a thermal column, hovering like a fighter jet. Rotating ads suggest that you take pictures in the Serengeti: see the last of the elephants, the last of the panthers, the last of the tigers. Injured passengers with broken legs or who can't make the long trek to departure gates are transported in carts pulled by Clydesdales. A victorious Brazilian football team writhes through transit like a colourful snake in the broken Amazon, brown bodies rubbing against large green leaves, singing West African music transformed during the early Atlantic crossings into Brazilian pop classics. Team colours on bags and suitcases and Swatches in bright colours. Loud South American laughter spreads among the citizens. The team salsas by and is replaced by overweight aboriginal Canadians returning from a victorious anti-racism *and* diabetes conference in Geneva. LHR-Toronto-Whitehorse. Harrods bags made from the finest painted flex cardboard jostle through. More pinpoints of light become inaudible screeches on the tarmac. Shopping bags and stars. Moslem clerics. Soft-palmed Buddhists. Defensive Sikhs, reluctant to answer questions—because they, on purpose, understand only Panjabi. Then, suddenly, a specific pinpoint of light appears in the distance. The flipping announcement board indicates a PIA flight, which, due to weather, has been redirected to LHR not Manchester where it was supposed to go. The plane floats down into the English night with its cargo of future cooks for south Asian restaurants in Brick Lane, South Hall, Glasgow, Perth, Aberdeen, and on the Isle of Jura. The evening clouds puff apart for the PIA flight that arrives on the nose from Islamabad at 19:37. Not late, but the wrong airport, and due only to a light Mancunian fog.

A horde of twenty-one Sumo wrestlers in black suits heaves into view and passes by in human knots of three.

One of the wrestlers is an African-American who is carrying a novel in his swollen hand. Four plump, ruddy middle-aged men in lederhosen read newspapers. The middle-aged men turn to look at Joseph. They are far from being Germanic. All these men in lederhosen are Japanese. They return to their Japanese papers. In Duty-Free, a gaggle of five fully covered Saudi women are buying perfume, alcohol, cartons of cigarettes. One accidentally brushes against a priest wearing a name tag: "Hello, I am Father Seenen. Catholic Convention of European Bishops, I-heart-symbol-Catholicism." Joseph notices twelve Catholic priests in frocks. They are buying scotch and chocolates with a credit card. A large backlit poster states *American Express Spoken Here*, with an imprint of the card and a name—not Joe Doe as in the old days, but Sham Neeladaria—and an expiration date.

From the café, Joseph notices her. Olive eyes set in Gothic East European skin: Gorgana Arabiyeva, who initially came to Europe via Padua or Venice, is wearing a tight, black mini-skirt and a grey leather jacket. Italy is the smugglers' gateway to western Europe. Turkey is the staging post for the Middle East, Gulf States, and Saudi Arabia where there is nothing but sand, and catholic rule upon catholic rule on how to live, and, rules on why one should not give one's self a breast examination, due to the risk of causing collateral sexual stimulation. She was on vacation and is going through the airport. She has a small suitcase beside her; she's just arrived from Malta. Her fingernails are painted a metallic grey and he thinks to himself that tomorrow she'll be wearing yellow gloves.

The green leaves of a palm tree droop over Joseph as he moves on his bench. He walks over to a fast-food stand. He takes a croissant and hot coffee and slowly eats. When he finishes, he walks toward the toilets. A sandwich board sign outside states: "Please excuse the inconvenience, this toilet is being cleaned."

Gorgana looks less glamorous in a cleaner's smock and yellow gloves. She enters the toilet with her mop and then stops awkwardly. "Excuse me sir," she says addressing Joseph, who is standing at the sink with his torso bare. Silently, he looks at her through the mirror. He has his earphones on and his hairy armpits are lathered up. They stare at each other. Joseph, expressionless, removes his earphones. "Brahms. Do you like Brahms?"

"I am sorry sir. I was closing the toilet for cleaning."

"It's okay," he replies. Gorgana nods and starts to walk out of the toilet.

Gorgana is momentarily distracted as she tries to replace a bottle of cleaner on a closet shelf. Accidentally, a thick cobalt blue cleaning chemical falls, making a flat pool on the floor. Gorgana steps outside, leaving the door propped open.

As Joseph walks past, his trolley makes a clicking sound because a piece of yellow packing tape is stuck to the right rear wheel. The sound is like a clock speeding up and slowing down. His hair is neatly combed. He passes through trolley noises, bits of conversations, dinging of cashier registers. He stops briefly and looks at the flight numbers, gates, boarding times, destinations, blinking, flashing, changing. He stares at the clock.

In Hebrew followed by French, the announcer states:

"Passengers for El Al flight 0916 are requested to go to gate J-6 for boarding." Joseph moves past gates A-13, A-14, A-15 without turning his head. At gate A-16, he stops and stares at the boarding counter of Icelandair. A green light flashing; the sign reads "Icelandair. Reykjavik. 08:35. Now Boarding". For a moment, Joseph is hypnotized by this sign.

A wet voice that trips on teeth informs passengers:

> *Flight 72 to Honolulu now boarding at gate B-48; Flight 0947 now boarding for Osaka. Will the following persons please come to the ticket counter: Vasu Makakungerbazi, Maeve Bligtonburgh, Pollycarp Dukaczewski, Julius Merodach, James Nguyen-Fitzgerald, James Aurignacia, Aziz al-Abub, Hussien Muhammad Fadallah, Sheikh Muhammad Hussein al-Mussawi, Sayyis Abub, Muhammad, Hussien Mussawi, Abdul el Guillotine, Mrs Tub Qwais Yannie, Oliver El Twist, Muhammad Aziz Muhammad, Sheikh Muhammad, Tony Malone, Kala Bazee, and Girja Muqudas Panee, El Outsider, and Safade Makudma.*

As he moves past flight gates B-5, B-7 et cetera, he sees the following: A school of veiled women loaded down with designer shopping bags. A tall, veiled woman stoops to pick up a package which has fallen out of her hand; he bends down to help her. She stares into his eyes; her eyes are surrounded by black cloth. Momentarily, he looks at her high-heeled sandaled foot with toenails painted silver-pink. He looks into her eyes. She stares back. Her shapely body is outlined by her devotion to Islam. He salaams the woman who, in a husky voice, *wa'aleekum salaams*. She continues smiling into his face. Rules are governed by geography: Jeddah is far away.

Day 3, 26 Dhul Hijjah 1408

This is an airport, not a Medina, Joseph thinks to himself. The strain of the wait is making it easy for him to imagine conversations in the whorling world of transit. He is now mildly paranoid. He imagines the following taking place deep inside the airport.

> *Dark suits meet: chief of Airport Police and an Airport Security Assistant et al. The French are in Heathrow to help with Joseph. Interpol also. Someone standing in front of an array of security monitors states: "Anglo-Saxon multiculturalism is not a threat to us. Liberty, Equality, Fraternity—it all started here, but will always remain French, messieurs. Clearly our times are more complex than the time of Zola and the rights of workhorses in mines. Modern liberalism, you see. We are highly tolerant, but there are laws for tolerance. You see?"*
>
> *The police chief responds: "Clearly: you suspect people of smuggling. Right here in this airport. Right here in Heathrow?"*

> *"We're not very demanding: a few arrests, the pawns will do. The airport's snakeheads."*
>
> *The assistant says: "It's always the pawns. And the fundamental problem persists."*
>
> *"We are here working with you English to stop European airports from being used like this."*
>
> *The Airport Security Assistant produces two passports and opens them up to a page and puts them in front of the Chief of Airport Police. He looks closely at the visa stamps. "Valid passports, valid visas. Not a trace ... we can't find these people anywhere. And, we have nothing on the Paki. We're going to let the wog go. We'll keep an eye on the cleaning woman. He chats with her. We have nothing on her either."*

"Last time: where are you from?"

Joseph hands him Lindy Goughagan's card.

They've caught him. A woman lawyer named Lindy Goughagan has flown in from County Cork to help free him from transit, and to free him from his lifelong membership on the cricket team. She, he imagines, wrote her doctorate on Cerebral Spinal Meningitis and something to do with refugees. She's a human rights lawyer who is tall, slender with black bangs across her forehead. An immigration official, who looks like a doctor, walks past him. A defeated-looking Asian refugee held by the arm is being walked down the hall. Could the official be a nurse or a doctor? An immigration official bluntly addresses Joseph.

"You're in shit," the official says as he walks out of the detention room.

As the door opens, the previously seen Asian refugee is being carried back by the armpits by two beefy security personnel. The Asian's body is flaccid, a yellow line of vomit runs down the front of his shirt. A balding, fat official walks in. He sifts through some of Joseph's objects which have been dumped into a plastic tray next to the briefcase. He notices an academic handbook of irrigation methods and an advanced calculator. Why is an immigration official wearing a stethoscope around his neck? Abruptly, he asks in Arabic: "How long have you been here? Egyptian? Lebanese? The Chouf Mountains? The Khyber Pass? The Alps, maybe? You're Hannibal? Back home you'd have talked by now."

Joseph is silent and thinks: Yes, back home, I'd have talked. The official points to a box of latex medical gloves on the table.

"Get your pants off. The doctor's going to examine you."

They leave him sitting. He falls into a mild sleep and is awoken when he hears one official ask another: "Where did he dig up a lawyer?"

Minutes later, Goughagan enters the room. She's in her forties, dressed in grey slacks and a dark blue jacket, and somehow, she looks familiar. Looking at the two immigration men, she states: "My client made no attempt to enter the United Kingdom. He has done nothing illegal."

"Madame Goughagan, before he became a citizen of our transit lounge, he was deported from Houston, four days ago."

The lawyer, who looks and seems like a doctor, says: "And so it's the business of the Americans."

The taller official pushes some papers across the table saying: "Who knows, perhaps the pilot was sympathetic? He gave him his papers and your client, who knows? He put them in the toilet. And now, Madame Goughagan, he's our problem. We intend to deport him."

"To where?" she asks.

"Home."

"Where do you estimate that is?" Goughagan asks.

The official says: "Slovakia. Where else?"

"My client is stateless."

"Nice word, *stateless*. The word means nothing."

Goughagan ignores his digression, pushes the paper back towards them saying: "Ask the Slovaks. No record of this man in their records, actually, and they don't want to take him. Under International Law, the UN is in charge of stateless people."

"The United Nations."

"Let me be clear: your examination of my client has been a violation."

The official, who hasn't said anything till now, asks in a French accent: "So you want us to accept him in England, as a friend of the prime minister's?"

"He should be admitted into England as a refugee," Goughagan says.

"He's not staying here," the man with the French accent says.

"He is not a threat. So until I have his papers straightened out, my client will wait in transit, which isn't strictly England."

"This is an airport not a medina," he replies.

A uniformed security man asks: "Madame Gough-agan, how long will this take?"

"Not long. Not long at all."

The official with the stethoscope looped around his neck asks: "So you used to play cricket?" I think that the memory pills are helping, don't you think so? Joseph, your health is good."

He laughs to himself. This is the imagination running on autopilot. This is the occupational risk of becoming a team captain.

A screen reveals Gorgana's hands sifting through Styrofoam cups and melted ice cream; wiping spilled drinks off the floor and a seat. The transit hall makes her look small. Un-evolving morning sunlight which looks grey in the video image, falls in transit. Gorgana reaches into rubbish bins and dumps the trash into the big sack on her trolley. She comes across a porn magazine. She briefly leafs through it before dumping it. She places a lost CD in her pocket. A colourful array of bottles and liquids jutting out like a city skyline rest on her cleaning trolley. After cleaning this section, Gorgana props a yellow plastic "Bathroom Cleaning" sign outside a toilet. The black and white monitor switches now to the internal scenes of the men's room: snowy black and white images of her cleaning a toilet.

Near LHR is a power plant, old deciduous trees, now *anthracite*, are being burnt to power the banks of security monitors inside the airport. The monitors send out images of life in Heathrow and life outside on the runways. A conspiracy of electronic images.

Day 4, 27 Dhul Hijjah 1408

Night. Joseph is watching the runway, hundreds of jumbo planes bounce up into the sky and drop down on the tarmac like wasps flying into a nest. The large planes leave beautiful trails across the early night sky. Over the span of a few seconds, he sees several sunsets, and several night falls; and the moon moves through its phases. He has memorized certain arrival and departure times: Cathay Pacific flight 447, arrival 21:22, gate C-34; Varig flight 1500 non-stop service to Rio, departure 22:00; All Concord passengers—pas de service pour le moment. PIA to Islamabad 18:57. Rapidly, a gibbous moon arcs into view lighting the airplanes as they land. Moonlight falls on the runways, all the planes, all the hangars.

He looks down and sees his bare feet in black and white flip-flops. He wonders if terrorists wear flip-flops.

He's walking to a toilet near the gate for an Australian airline. As he nears the boarding gate, he hears accents that sound like sheep drowning in the lower cargo holds of a sinking ship. Nearby, he hears two Glaswegians with Amaryllian voices, farther away, he hears orchestral Basque. Outside, four Rolls Royce engines whine, pushing a defiant old jumbo out to runway C-47 and up into the elements.

The events of the near future will change his life. Will he integrate into the English world of terrorists? Could it be his last day in transit? Not even the Icelandair 747 carrying two icebergs on its wings will pull him away from his goal. Will he think of icebergs again in his life? *Will he ever see real icebergs?* He pushes the white door open, walking into the world of the international airport toilet, where the urines of Ulan Bator and Madrid mix. A man in a blue suit, arched backwards, is pissing in a far urinal. He's young, so his piss is audible, splattering out like a brook at springtime. From the small bag on his trolley he reaches into a black sports bag, pulling out a Ziploc bag. A diminished bar of blue Irish Spring falls out of his hand and into the hot water. He leans forward, and raises his left arm and rubs soap into his right armpit, being a man of balance, he repeats the action on the other side. With a glance into the mirror, he bends over the sink and washes the soap off. He washes his feet, one leg up at a time. He's not a Moslem. He's not anything. The blue suit walks out. Joseph cleans the sink with paper towels. Again, he catches sight of himself in the mirror and asks himself: Where will I grow old? Where will I live? He pulls himself near the surface of the mirror. Eyes look into the mirror-illusion of eyes. Is the eye not an object in its own field? He notices black bits of facial hair resting in a spiral bed of soap suds in the sink. He turns on the cold water and with open palms washes his dead skin and hair into England.

Joseph stops and stares at the fluttering announcements board. The name of his home town flutters up and holds for a few seconds, then flutters into Beziers.

He can feel that the fat man with a round nose is going home to Cleveland. Most fat people who visit Europe are Americans.

He is preoccupied with being detected. What will they ask? Where was he born? What's he doing in transit for a few days? It isn't normal to wait in transit? Can he tell them where he's from? A place where a vivisection of the state took place in 1947? Or perhaps a liberation in 1971? Perhaps Marshal Tito, born on the 7th of May, was the head of his state. When he was younger, airplanes dropped chemicals on his uncles, who moved all the time. What, imprecisely, could he tell anyone questioning him?

At the café where Joseph spends some time the TV volume is loud. The sound of church bells is loud. Joseph has to raise his voice to be heard. Pierre says: "The Pope's in paradise."

"I had no idea. I'm sorry."

They both look at a plume of black smoke rising from the Vatican. The CNN journalist states: "Black smoke means that the 120 sequestered cardinals have not yet elected a new Pope. The question burning in everyone's mind in Anno Domini something something is: Will the cardinals elect the first gay Jamaican supreme pontiff of the universal church?"

Pierre, the restaurateur, comments: "Good smoke," switches channels to a documentary on the sex trade. The TV journalist states: " ... 300,000 women and young girls, smuggled through the Balkans and Turkey, work in the sex industry in Western Europe." The TV channel is switched back to the black plume of smoke.

Again, he notices more passengers: a Bolivian woman with a round face wearing a bowler hat; a fifty-year-old man whose beard covers his face; a Turkish Sufi with a droopy face and a surging beard wearing a robe of many colours.

From a telephone booth he calls Gorgana.

A male voice says: "Hello."

"Hello. Do I have 40 17 89 00 89, Gorgana. Please."

In the distance, Gorgana is informed about the call; Londonistani sounds in the background. Gorgana is now on the phone. "Hello."

"Hello."

"Joseph?" Gorgana asks.

"Yes, Usha. Thanks for your help." Joseph calmly hangs up.

He trolleys away. A rotating advertising column—one of the ads is for a safari park outside a city—turns to reveal an image of the earth in black space: "interstellar banking." Two passengers have hot towels over their faces. They remove them in unison. They are identical twins. Joseph is sitting near them in a row of passengers.

Day 5, 28 Dhul Hijjah 1408

Joseph is now going for a sink shower. Beside him, a suit is washing up. Calmly, Joseph stuffs the old shirt in the rubbish bin and puts on a clean white shirt and dabs on aftershave which is also tossed into the rubbish. He parts his hair on the left side. He starts to throw things from his trolley into the trash and heads off to Bon Voyage.

He's at the Air Malta gate. He is waiting, groomed, ready for London. He walks past the boarding gate when passengers flow out.

After brushing past each other in front of McDonald's, Gorgana takes Joseph to the underground cargo bay. They walk under the noisy water pipes bolted to the concrete ceiling.

A friend within the airport has had the security cameras in this section turned off for repairs. The long corridor leads to a cargo storage area which is flooded with sodium lights. A cage in the corner contains two large black panthers. Panther number one is still in a daze. Panther number two has defeated the tranquillizer and is pacing back and forth. Number two gives a slow rolling growl, stretches and peers out at Gorgana and Joseph.

"Where are they going?"

Gorgana points to the waybill taped to the cage. Shanghai Zoo, Customs clearance: 1C948R8491. China Air. "But not really to a zoo." She snips the air with her fingers like chop sticks. Joseph looks away and imagines what the panthers have been through:

> *We met one day at an inter-species supper. She has melanistic colouration just like mine, black and shiny. Now, she's sleeping. Can't wait to see her yellow eyes again. They were filled with tropical sunshine when I last saw them. We were walking near a lagoon not far from the river. Originally, we're from farther north: we live near where we can smell the field workers, farmers and their cows and goats. Sometimes, the dust mixes with the rain and we can see mud stuck in their cloven hooves. When we hear voices we move away until the sun drops, then we can do what we like.*
>
> *The afternoon rain tapers. Now, a few drops fall from the larger leaves. I lick the white clouds reflected in the lagoon. She's noticed the goat's*

smell. I keep trying to get in between the goat and her. The smell isn't moving, this means that the goat is not moving. My friend pretends that I've haven't noticed her pointing her nose in that direction. She smiles at me as we drink. I claw her thigh.

The goat is no longer present in her mind, I think. But wait, the goat is now in her mind. In fact her mind is now filled with goat. The goat's left or right nostril is clogging with fresh blood; someone's done that with a razor so that we'd smell both the blood and the piss. The topmost leaves on the tree shake. The twine—cat-gut, made from one of us—will not break. The more she thrashes the tighter it gets. The goat knows we're waiting. A nose dripping blood on the green leaves.

My friend steps into an anthill, she shakes them off and pushes her open claws into the jungle.

The hunters are using something that covers their odour or makes them smell like blue parrots after a rain shower. Overhead, a large parrot screeches. The afternoon is becoming early evening.

She thinks if we don't act now, the other panthers will eat the goat and we'll suck on entrails. I try to keep her mind on the white clouds reflected in the water. I lick her long body, trying to get her mind out of the trap. I've succeeded in distracting her? No. She's trembling. Okay, we'll walk past the goat, just one circle. Just to see if it's safe. She bites my neck. I growl. The entire area is now fearpissed. A radar-driven idiotic fruit bat stirs from slumber. I try to reach for it. This makes her laugh. A python with yellow triangles on its sides elongates up a tree so he can better see what's about to happen.

Goat. Mind. Goat. No mind, just goat. What season are we in? Plenty of four-legged food around. We both know it's a trap, so let's walk away from it. How will we know it's a trap if we don't test it? What if we go there and rip the goat to shreds and nothing bad happens to us? Dinner with blood.

A breeze moves the clouds away from the surface of lagoon. The idea of piss converts into hairy surface flesh, bone, muscles, and veins, squirting blood, fat. We'll gnash away at its gums and chew off the knuckles. We'll bite her neck bringing departure within seconds. Squirt. I hear blood evaporating off the edge of her lips.

Leaves as big as parachutes dither in the sunlight. I see the blue gun turning white in the sun. What are they using these days? I am thirty years old. I've seen everything. I've survived. I can't smell them and the wind is coming from their direction.

Like lizards, we drag down on the jungle floor, hearts going like mad. We're in this together. What's a trap? We'll kill the hunters—it'll be across the Daily Panther by sun up. Black Panthers kill two white hunters and eat goat: Heroes.

Our whiskers touch. We kiss. They can tell we're nearing: the anxiety of the stupid little piebald goat, ballerina panic ears flapping, rib cage hammering against the tree, is now evident to the entire jungle. Its eyes bulge when she feels my friend nearing, grass tenderly conforming to her body like waves in a warm sea. I laugh at the goat bashing its sides against the banana tree. We both remember the motto of all panthers: meat on the outside becomes meat on the inside.

Tangled in more twine. We tire out the goat by just being there. Broken streams of piss run down her leg. Fear governs us all: the scentless hunters, the goat, us. Love binds us. My gracious panther—queen of the jungle—circles the goat. I crawl behind her, pissblood everywhere in the air. She's going to claw her bladder first. I have my partner's bum in front of my face, moving, and I'm supposed to be hunting.

Eye-to-eye: the goat is dead still, as though a plot has suddenly been bared and the actors have come to the stage's edge. A banana falls on its head. We laugh. Poor little goat. I'm in the tall jungle grass hoping they will not see us and that we'll soon have goat blood all over our mouths. So, hunter, where's your trap? My friend stops and raises her head. She feels the trap around us. If this desire is not the trap then what is?

A dart politely sinks into her sweaty neck. She's twitching like the goat now, sleep comes to her. The goat is balancing the banana on her head. My love and devotion propel me toward my panther. Of course I'll share her fate. An insignificant bee stings me. What's a mother and father? We ate a gazelle at New Year's at Kampala four months ago. Our yellow eyes shut instantly. I dream about the farmers and their cows. My paw touches her neck, and I dream about our walks in the forest. Who is going to feed our baby panthers in our lair? My mother and father are distant memories.

I hear the sound of cars on a broken road, then echoing voices in a large room. We are in a cool space with no lights. My chest hurts. There's a large bottle with a tube. Suck tube equals water. We can figure it out. It's dark. I can taste the chemical in my mouth. We hear a screech and then our cage shakes and then we can't feel any motion. I see harsh daylight. I smell air that I've encountered on the clothes of Europeans. We're on a cart of some kind.

There are airplanes everywhere and men walking around holding yellow pads in their hands. Eyes everywhere. Yellow eyes. I'm not scared. I'm a panther. What do these airplanes know? We're now in a room with large lights on the ceiling. I'm more or less awake, but my friend's still sleeping: she must have received the same dose although she's smaller. A slip of paper hanging on our cage states: Shanghai Zoo, and various numbers attached to customs and veterinarian export papers. We're going there by China Air.

I hear a door open. Two people walk toward our cage. I let out a big growl to scare them. But it comes out as the growl of a young cub. She has the nerve to touch my paw through the bars. I order my claws out to harm her, but only another cub growl leaves my mouth, that's how weak I've become.

I have strength enough to pace in the tiny cage. A tired looking man with a day's beard says to the woman touching me: "Gorgana, what's this? Where are they going. Are they for the London Zoo? How nice of you to bring me here, to cargo."

She has on a pale blue dress and a scarf on her head. I can smell human piss on her, but no fearpiss. Why all the piss smell? She can't keep her eyes off me. She's drawn to me. Let me look at her before my friend wakes up. I snarl at her again. She loses herself in my eyes. I could claw her wrist off for touching me. I've set a trap for her. I ignore the man who looks like he's never seen a beautiful black panther.

"It looks like they are going to the Shanghai Zoo. China Air," she says. He asks: "Is there a shortage of tigers in China?"

"They're not tigers, Joseph."

"Well then, they are cats or jaguars? I know they like to live near water. How did they arrive here I wonder?"

"Do you have zoos where you come from?" he asks her.

"They're not really going to a zoo. You know that, don't you?"

Gorgana imitates chop sticks with her fingers. "Endangered delicacies. Panther sauté with garlic served with deep-fried rat."

My lover opens her eyes. At once, she notices the female. We're leaving for China. We've got to escape, but how? I lick her face, her legs her breasts in front of the female. No one thinks about the man who doesn't move much. I think I'm licking the clouds in the lagoon where we roamed free. They stay and chat between themselves. They mention a man called Mohammad. We see daylight again moving on a cart toward an airplane. Darkness for a long time. We drink more water from the tube. They give us cow which tastes like it's been dead for a long time. We hear the same screech of large parrot followed by a hard thud. We land in a city in South China, our Kenyan ears can't understand the language, but I can smell familiar odours. We are taken to a large market where they transfer us into two smaller cages. I cry out to her. They keep us together but in separate cages. They don't put too much distance between us. Someone shows money. My head is pulled out of the cage with large metal pliers and a large hammer hits my skull and eyes. My body writhes in pain, but I'm not scared. I'm a black panther, even lions fear me. Supportively, my friend hisses. She's in the cage nearby and one of my eyes is knocked out. From my neck to my groin and all along my legs, the Chinaman tears off my skin in one respectful piece. It appears to me that the Chinaman is asking me the same questions again and again. I understand a few African languages but not Chinese. Chinese is not an African language. Someone yells Chinese words into my cage; I let the words into my mind. I think. I fully understand him: I'm a dead and an alive cat at the same time; I can have his language go inside me as Chinese and in my mind it becomes comprehensible Kenyan English. But he can't convert my colonial English into Chinese, hence the impolite departure of my limbs.

I growl out that I don't know what is he talking about. He keeps mentioning someone called Mohammad, then he throws my skin in hot water and someone stirs it and they pull it out to show the smiling crowd. He asks:

Mohammad made you do it? A music group is playing tweety opera nearby. Mohammad made you do it? He asks again and again. The rendition of music mixes with me saying: No I *don't understand the question but the stranger does not stop making the same sounds with his mouth. With a large knife he deeply pre-cuts but does not remove my legs. Deep gashes ready for the final blow when someone buys a part of me. Immediately, my paws have been chopped off and sold. I'm still alive, and my heart still beating in my open panther's chest. I can see it all from up here. There's a hook in the back of my neck and now I'm looking down at the people making a fashion statement with parts of my body. I'm hooked high above, and I can see all the empty ambition. I fix on someone who has paid for my right paw. My remaining eye follows him until he is out of the market. A full moon, begging for immigrants, glows in the sky. This is the night market. The Chinaman looks back at me.*

She won't last the afternoon. Someone has bought my leg. And another person is buying her. When they come for her she pulls back into the cage and cries like a hungry cub. The butcher, who's wearing wet, black rubber boots, pours scalding hot water on her back making her hiss and turn on her back, claws extended against the bamboo bars. The shoppers laugh at her. Her total skin leaves in one flawless, slow removal. Paws are hacked off and sold first.

I would do it again. There is nothing better than a trap to take you somewhere else. One trap leads to another. I am not very conscious. They bring me down and place me face up on a splendid bed of blood-red ice and rice. I look at white clouds in an evening sky. My pain has gone.

Gorgana opens the cage. The panthers have been Mohammad and Mohammad all along. Dressed as panthers, so to speak, Gorgana and Joseph escort them to the door that leads to transit and to the exit. Upright, they walk calmly. Two airport security men chuckle at Mohammad and Mohammad. At arrivals-and-departures none of the social antics they see everyday surprise them. A few travellers look and laugh also. Mohammad and Mohammad, remove their costumes and, with Joseph, flag a taxi into London with a view to causing as much damage as possible.

As the years passed, they did event after event, champagne corks going into orbit after each celebration. They remained undetected, causing terrific, cosmic disturbances which left England frightened and trembling as never before. Solar flames to right the wrongs. Their work was appreciated by every cave-dweller in Afghanistan, and provoked leading members of the Irish Republican Army, Euskadi Ta Askatasuna, (ETA) et al., to ask themselves: Why hadn't they thought of doing what the young Moslems are now doing? Wouldn't they have arrived at the table of endless negotiation centuries earlier? How large was their budget and who supplied them?

Why couldn't they as young men have done things of equal yet Irish scale?

And how on earth did Joseph and his group remain undetected? They remained undetected due to the long gaps between events; they remained undetected due to their conception of time.

Must time have a stop?

They went silent, at least for England they went silent. Learning to go under for years, or a decade is an art. One has to submit income tax, shop, cook, take kids on vacation, buy a birthday present, throw a *davat* for a few friends and so on, and so: via an agreement with funders dx, dy and dz, they did one last bang and boom in the United Kingdom, and went to Canada, via ship no less. Look out Canadians. They settled in cities, hopping from one to another—they did a few things which were useful in the larger balancing out of things. Bien sûr, a majority of Canadians were against what they did, let there be no doubt. The IDF recruits in western countries. Some Canadians joined them, but given the task at hand, only a minority. Then, suddenly, at the speed of an equatorial sunset, they, as a group, grew old. What follows is an epistle to imperialism and its sons.

4

Christopher Marlowe, Muharram

From up here on the hillside, I can see not only the large old folks home where I live but also my life in bits and pieces. As I walk down the path, the shape of the river changes. Snow covers the branches of the pine trees, and across the broad river bank are small purple hills. Muharram, in Québec, is the cruellest month. The pills doctors give me cause my memories to flood back with precision, without guilt or arrogance. The fresh winter air has, now and then, tinges of the smell of airport transit lounges, where I've spent much time. Through the cold, stark branches in Pierrefonds, I can see us at the table.

I remember a handful of men and women in our younger bodies, eyes aflame—in our English house outside London. Was it near Hayes and Harlington? At the table, we, the really committed few, have the almost odourless Semtex. Or was it Pentaerythritol tetranitrate that our friends purchased, via a Scottish South Asian proxy, in the Czech Republic?

I turn my head in the direction of Montreal. As the wind purrs through the near and faraway trees, I remember the plush governmental Westminster tube stop. As Big Ben strikes in London, a black crow in Pierrefonds lifts into the air. A plume of serpent smoke in Arabic lettering issues from Russell Square. What a heavenly pleasure it is to see Bloomsbury in Mumbaian panic. Momentarily, and for days afterwards, we've throttled the city of Christopher Marlowe and his Moslem of Malta. But all that's in our vainglorious past.

We didn't do any of it. We're innocent. *I count religion but a childish toy, And hold there is no sin but ignorance.*

The snow covered path takes me nearer to the old folks home. I am now right on the hillside, not near Westminster. The flat ice will remain in that state until March, when, according to my epiphanic opinion a state-shift will take place: 13 March Anno Domini something something. I'm now decaying near Montreal. I'm a terrorist—non-convicted, thus innocent, thus a free citizen, thus a near-free citizen swaddled in the white cloth of occidental tyranny. Who these days isn't a terrorist? One man's terrorist is another man's old folks home friend; one man's terrorist is another's transit lounge passenger.

Black trees shimmer against the setting sun. The home is a two-storey assembly in the shape of a large X, eighty by eighty metres, surrounded by acres of trees and snow-covered lawns. The path up to where I am now has only a mild incline for someone of my physical strength.

My hearing aid contains my entire archive of music, from childhood to my forthcoming grave, forthcoming. Semi-classical Indian music, Ustad Amjad Ali Khan, blends with the Kurdish woodwinds in the spruces and the rustling of my ultra lightweight black down coat.

The door to the institution's kitchen has been left open. A phone rings, pots rubbing against large metal sinks, the sound of cutlery hitting a water-filled plastic bucket, the voices of two young kitchen helpers, and a woman with a deep voice. I can hear the sound of a chemical-loaded steel-wool pad rubbing against pots; the sound of a swirling water galaxy, I can visualize bits of broccoli and water-soaked Uncle Ben's rice flowing down the drain in a taut spiral. Pills for hearing. Broccoli for farting.

I stop, stoop, and look at the lower branches of one of the trees near me. I single out one branch for staring —to look at the pine needles, the deep green. I shut my eyes and I hear the sounds of the kitchen again. Through the double glass doors I walk into the home and head to my room. The tungsten bulbs fill the rooms with a yellowish light. It becomes black and silent for a few hours, then the orchestra warms up: the rumble of an early morning landing place awakens me. We're in their path. A woman is vomiting feculently. What's her name? She can't be the woman in the airport, can she? That woman I knew? No. This is someone different. Is her name Jennifer? She is connected with us. She comes and goes. Today, she is shouting with a dry voice, catches her breath and then the dark liquid leaves her mouth. She pants, refills her lungs, makes more dry sounds. I know her. I'll invite her to my birthday party. If she gets better. She has vascular diseases, diabetes, atherosclerosis, osteoporosis, mild cognitive impairment, a caloric intake of one thousand per day, cancer. But no memory loss. Pleasant ending she'll have. The flesh pads on the soles of her feet are non-existent because she doesn't eat. A nurse calms her. Someone is cleaning a bathroom. I remember someone in my life who cleaned washrooms. Another phone rings in the distance. A guilt-ridden son or daughter?

The central nurse's station is situated at the confluence of these halls. There is an elevator at the end of the north-south hallway that takes us one floor up for X-rays and small operations such as brain transplants. I'm not going there today. I'm sitting on the lawn, or rather on the lawn chair, which itself is sitting on the lawn. I know I have a visitor today.

Faintly, in the background, I hear Bobby Darin's hit "Dream Lover." I've never gotten used to dealing with criminal investigating types. Why? I've never been questioned. I've been wondering what that would be like.

Divinely, we've spun into a sunny late morning between breakfast and lunch. I'm sitting at the end of the hall with a window looking out over the lawn and the river. A police detective approaches me in a humble European walking style. Thank you for the call. You're here about the London story? I ask myself, he did call today, didn't he? And was it about the London story or am I just suffering from narcissism?

They say my memory is now hyperthymestic. My nurse, Linda, leans toward my ear: "Dr. Macleod, good morning, a man is here to see you. He said that he'd already spoken with you on the phone. Do you remember I told you yesterday?"

"Please tell him I'll meet him inside." A tall man with a moustache who is trying to look like a police detective approaches me at a table on the sunny lawn. Or is it Anver dressed up? Interesting to have visitors. I can see and faintly hear the bowling balls clink each other in the background, behind the glass. I sip at white institutional china cups of tea with milk.

"Hello, Dr. Macleod, thanks for making the time to see me, please don't get up."

"Pleasure's all mine, thanks for your call. Have a seat."

"This is a lovely place." He's looking softly yet directly at my eyes, then glances over at the elderly hands slowly rolling balls on green grass.

Joseph Macleod was the organizational brains behind it all. I keep him entertained with mannered panic.

"Diaries? Who wrote these diaries? I've haven't heard of them before. I was the brains behind the events—proof? Sounds like I'll have to defend myself in court. Who's reopened the case? I ask as I look out at the rheumatoid bowlers. Is the word Diaries a code for something? I don't sense cop, I really don't sense cop. Why would they try to contact me now after all these years of silence?"

After pausing, I continue: "By the way, you're not a journalist. What are you? You're a mystery man, a writer? So much excitement in the winter of my uric boredom, who would have thought." He appreciates my sense of humour.

"I'm just a freelance journalist, nothing more exotic than that, I'm afraid." We both know why he's here, so we continue playing.

"Journalist. Right. What else do you want to ask me?"

Someone is trying to prove me guilty or should I say consult me on the affair after so many years. "Tell me, what's the importance of it all now?"

"I need some points in the story fleshed out. On the surface, it looks like a simple act carried out by the same people who did subsequent flash-and-bangs. Or was it someone else? Many governments are thought to have cooperated."

"Supposition. I don't think you're writing a book ... Governments, plots? Old-fashioned all that. I think it was an act of generalized Islamic guidance. All I've ever done, and I maintain it to this day, is play a flaccid literary critic of western imperialism. Now, if you have proof to the contrary, tell me or the courts. I'm enjoying our conversation."

My visitor leaves. Or is it Anver playing a trick on me? A trick yes, but one with my agreement? Testing for leaks. Is this trick a dry run-through in case someone comes asking questions? We almost had a release of information from our Irish helper. But somehow she died before she could talk. Some of us, when we get older, feel bad about what we did and want to talk about it. I'm here to die as well as to make sure that there is no flow-out.

The man says he'll come back, and I say: "Please do —it's really been a pleasure to have been stimulated in this way. Otherwise, my mind could become one of the balls on the green. You've saved my mind from becoming a ball with holes in it. Thank you very much."

He hands me his card. I notice his name on the card, Jamal Masoume—a son of one of our partners. He does not notice the joyous shudder that goes through me. Why is the son of a past project manager coming to see me? Anver with a wig? Anver becomes Jamal. This happens when I'm in between cycles of taking my modern pills.

Sequences of events go awry. Dress rehearsal. Canadian authorities. You see this is what happens in old age: one person becomes another and when they become another they get to wear all this intellectual decoration that can make them into Dimitris or Mohammads. All Dimitris evolve from Charlemagne.

In old age they can become Jamal Masoumes from the world over—they can become Anver playing detective, making sure there are no leaks. They can become dancers at the Lincoln Centre who don't point their toes like in the old days in Moscow. All's possible in the old age that terrorists live through. The anti-aging mental drugs make us alert.

I walk along a hall. I see Nurse Linda in the background. Gladly, she's within earshot of this memorable rendezvous which, I'm calculating, will draw us closer together. Closer, but no cigar. I've no illusions. The Man says: "Thanks, yes, I'd like more tea."

"Looks like a planned event with a heavy government subsidy," I say, then pause for drama. The Man-who-looks-like-a-police-detective-but-isn't fills my afternoon with questions that take practically no thought to answer. I get up and mimic his European walk down the East-West hall past a series of windows that open onto a lawn that merges with the water. I live in fear of deathbed confessions from my tribe.

5

Diary

I'm thinking about a woman I met here in the home. Was she my wife? Did my wife die in Paris, London or Pierrefonds? Did she die in a hospital—near rue de Tombe-Issoire? But this is not about her. I hear my past. I say: "Taxi, taxi." I notice the young Algerian driver. In Arabic, I respectfully ask: "Can you take me to Sailkot?" The taxi driver thinks for a moment, smiles, and says: "Bien sûr, Monsieur, avec plaisir, Monsieur." He respects me because I'm older. We've a long drive ahead of us. His name wanders out—Salah—from Wilaya quatre or cinq, Alger.

I start to talk without being asked. "They didn't drive me out, I left of my own free will—s'dit immigration. Left where? Doesn't matter where; I remember details: who came; why they came; who left; when they left; when the cobbler's son died; the invasions."

He listens *comme un initié*. I have the taxi driver in my world. "I've lived here for twenty-five years. My daughters are married, except one ... except one, look here she's at the pyramids at Giza. I think we had twins. They were good at cricket—that's what someone told me." We move south-west along the river. His hands move in circles over the steering wheel; the river, bright with sodium lights, disappears as we round a corner. He falls into my story because he's too young to have one of his own. A traffic light blares green. Olive groves; roasting lamb at a noisy wedding; the '67 borders; the behaviour of Jewish Canadian tourists in Jerusalem.

Salah, the taxi driver, gently brakes in front of a police station. I worked for Banque Oussman, Misr, L'egypte, yannie. My driver knows there isn't a village called Sailkot near here. Sailkot isn't a village anymore.

"Monsieur, your kids might be looking for you. Please enter and tell the police who you are so your family can come and pick you up, s'il vous plaît." Smiles of a lost son. In a hushed voice, I say: "Take me to the airport. I can't die here."

Sailkot touches him. I step out of the cab and enter the glass doors and walk into the airport: but there is hush in this airport. I don't see flights and departure screens; I see trays with medicines arranged in rows. I see strange airline stewards—they look more like nurses. And the only pilots I can spot are ones with green overalls and large plastic tags hanging from their necks. Where am I? In an old folks home or at a friend's high-rise in downtown Montreal? We're surrounded by off-white walls with paintings. A large seascape hangs on the wall facing a window that gives a complete view over the mountain rising in the centre of Montreal. I lift up a cup of tea in the home, in my room, in front of the river, and put it down in Linda's apartment in front of the mountain covered with summer trees. Mount Royal Park in the clear blue air. On the wall a poster of a Franz Kline painting called *Elizabeth* or something like that.

In my room, two burgundy Persian carpets with dark green borders hang on either side of a large picture window. The snow outside is framed by black Arabic calligraphy. But am I in my room in the old folks home or am I visiting Linda at her house in the Plateau-Mont-Royal? Linda looks after us in this section of the home. It's my job to be needy. I'm listening to the radio. 13:00 hours Greenwich Mean Time. Welcome to Books and their Meanings ... Linda keeps asking me questions. We've become friends. Sometimes, she says she knows what I'm thinking. Here's what I am thinking now: Did the announcer's voice grow up in County Tyrone reading Joyce and the lesser Catholics? Did the voice have a blue-eyed mother from Zimbabwe and a black father from Hackney? Or did our newscaster grow up in southern Alberta with contemplative mountains? Obviously, the newsreader's accent is geo-linguistically unclear yet understandable. These words are new to her. She's paid to tolerate class imbalance. I bring my old shortwave radio nearer my ear, a thin blue antenna wire trailing on the carpet. A little distance away, the others continue in humble, diminutive conversation. To the best of our abilities, we all know each other. We all live in separate rooms. Every week someone dies. Every week one of us connected with the events dies.

I'm wearing a blue blazer, open collar, and stiff black jeans to impress the girls. Everyone plays cards. Complacent grey fools in computerized luxury wheelchairs, playing cards. I can hear the cards falling on the table. I can shower with my hearing aid in. Nothing happens, no sudden bursts of lightning in the brain. Water is an excellent conductor of electricity, but this is the twenty-first century and for all I know water may no longer conduct electricity. Anything can happen. My eyesight is as sharp as a bird's, no floaters.

In a corner, beside a rubber plant that has a graft attached to one of its branches, Abgail Connolly or Usha —can't remember who—speaks into the phone and then hangs up. I know about grafts. A few seconds later, it rings. Must be a guilty son. Linda watches me put the radio on the small table beside the green sofa.

I leave for a wee walk but am back with the old folks again listening to old shortwave radio. The static-filled BBC broadcast lingers in my mind like Acute Lymphoblastic Leukemia. Was it fair to calibrate all assassins in such a manner? Could the powers that be be doing all this again? Imagine Europe without the injection of Islamic civility—perennially dank caves without any knowledge of the Greek or African worlds. Most of the population of Europe is now over seventy years of age. Immigration has slowed down to a trickle. The Grey Race dominates Europe. Fascist Grey and the Grey of the Magna Carta, a grey whose face we kicked in. Imagine France without hairy Islamic football players. No World Cups. Even the Micronesians could beat them.

Anver is interested in my diary. I wonder if he'd be interested in reading this part? I'm not sure he'd get the sense of humour—sort of like that cab driver in Paris who took me to the police station instead of CDG—he had virtually no sense of humour. Anver moves beside me on the large couch. We are old *and* physically fit. We use computers, we drive cars, we take trains to downtown Montreal, and now, I split my virtual screen into two blocks and with my fingers move the screen in front of him and we start reading together. Anver says that it's nice that technology brings us together. He politely asks: "Why is this bit called 'Radius Islamicus' and why did we, or should I say you, add the long line: 'A submission to the Home Secretary?'"

Anver leans closer to my shoulder and peers into the screen. No one else is around so we tell the computer to voice it. We've selected English with a West Yorkshire accent—just so it sounds like our Mullah from the north country, and we've also selected a background sound to the reading—that crackly sound of a shortwave radio announcing that we had done some terrible things.

> *I, Joseph Macleod, QC, of an origin that could place my birth somewhere between the ancient city of Anchorage and Halabja, have been commissioned by the Home Office to submit to the public the narrative of events that led up to the attacks by four of us on London's very public places, buses on such and such a date, which I can't remember now. Perhaps I was off my memory pills for another two-week cycle. This investigation will be based on all of the evidence the government had, or is now currently compiling. I state unequivocally that I have neither consulted documents related to national security, nor files or documents related to international security. At the time of this writing, the events of London will not be brought before a public inquiry.*

Anver asks: "This is what you spend your time on?"

One of our training mullahs had a poetic way with Arabic, Urdu or Dari, or Pushtu or some other language—not the aforementioned—spoken around Eastern Anatolia.

Terrorists are like seawater droplets from the Bay of Biscay. They lift upwards, forming clouds that float over the grape growing regions, past the Isles of Scilly, past the towns of Land's End: Looe, Mevagissey, Mousehole, Newquay, Penzance, St. Ives and finally fall over Heathrow, drenching it with an embroidered water lace. A white plane loaded with 800 passengers was glistening in the drops of Atlantic water. Flight delayed. Inside, an old partner, arms akimbo says: "Imran, put this CD on the intercom."

As I look back on this operation from my old age, I remember Anver was a tall man. He was also an Islamic team player who liked geriatric music. He's slightly shorter now. "Bus Stop" by The Hollies, I remember this song spreading through the fuselage's cathedral-high ceiling. The song, once on "Top of the Pops," now, decades later wafting among the stiff blue flight attendants who wear tops that flare out from their waists. Over The Hollies, someone with a Yorkshire accent states: "Due to H5N1 we won't be serving chicken." Some passengers laugh—

maybe they didn't laugh. Women, children and the old being slowly let out in groups of two after ten minute intervals. An old man says he was in Auschwitz. A fellow operative, with prodigal affection, leads him off the plane.

Anver, with his aged brown face and white hair, says: "What is this, stand up terrorism? Who's going to think this is funny? You're making fun of our operation. Perhaps you're feeling guilty? I'm not. There is too much talk of planes in this story. You really want a plane on every page? Do you think we should invite Linda to come and listen to your diary? She might have fun with us?"

"Anver, listen."

Michel Imran Aflaq and the others will escort you to the toilet and back, if you want to go. Leave the door open. We have twenty minutes before we get our turn to take off. The Northern Line from Finsbury Park was late. Holburn was a mess, the Piccadilly line to Heathrow was late; hence, you are being subjected to delayed terror.

Anver pretends he is snoring. Silently, I wag my finger at him and restart *Radius Islamicus*:

We had been asked by the Lahori mullahs to look at new and unusual targets, with detailed plans and photos.

"But they weren't from Pakistan; they were something else," Anver says.

"What were they then? Listen for a while." I wind back a few seconds so Anver can keep it all linked.

> *We had been asked by the various mullahs who visit England from time to time to look into underground tube stops. So, we went underground. While western democracy was licking its wounds and the cultural intellectuals wrote novels and articles about non-state actors and their relationship to Islam, Imran and others were sent to calculate tube stops worldwide. What's a graduate doing in a job like this, you're asking yourselves? You're most likely thinking: Will you be knapsacked in the air, or the sea or on the beaches, or right here en route to the runway? We've manners and we're rational, as rational as your white heads of states. We thought a great deal about viral and bacterial matters but most of us had educations in numbers and not chlorophyll-related stuff and synthetic biologically related class-struggle tools. In hindsight, this was not good. Some of us had long discussions on botulinum neurotoxin, ricin, tetrodotoxin, and other such things, but the institutional atmosphere within biology departments was so alien to us that we stuck to literature, history, and numbers.*

In the vast and airy cabin all were now silent with their collective worries. Seat belt lights off. Why worry? You all look so terrorized. We're just taking you in another direction from the one you planned on taking. Simply changing direction doesn't make us terrorists, does it? We are accelerants, not terrorists, aren't we?

We learnt our customs not only from hills and dales in the sweet-smelling English countryside, from Hadrian's Wall, and the moors, but also from the culture at large. So we'll be polite with you. We won't change your biological status, don't worry. That's what you're worried about, isn't it? Biological changes that we might bring about against your will? We will be leaving Heathrow in a few moments. Against your will. Just before we get going ... this is going to sound flaky, I know, but we have a psychologist with us; she is an Islamic psychologist—not veiled, of course—her name is Usha and she's a Sufi-Freudian and is willing to explain to you why this isn't an interpretation of a bad dream but actually a reality that you are now in. Maybe your pre-hijacking reality was a dream. She is willing to talk to you one on one. Some of you might need that kind of attention. At any rate, ponder these questions as we fly. Moreover, just to prove that we are not against Jews, we have asked all Jews to leave this flight. The last thing we want is to make this a flying Auschwitz and have the media represent us as people who dislike Jews. I hope this changes your impression. If you have a name that is not Jewish, then you stay. Is this clear? If you pretend that you have a Jewish name and try to leave without our permission, we might make changes to your outward morphologyberg with this thing that I have in my hand. We will be flying at a super low altitude from here to Cairo—this will prevent armed interruption from nations. So sit back, let your respective governments worry about you, and for now enjoy the view of cities and landscapes. For the Catholics among us—we'll go over the Vatican. Don't forget to tell the media that we showed respect for your idiotic belief systems. Some passengers turn their heads to look at landing planes. Thai Airlines moves toward the terminal to discharge passengers. Asian passengers swine-nosed to the windows, appear to be watching the unfolding drama but aren't aware of it.

A little bit about me: I come from a mid-sized city somewhere in the Midlands. In this city, I frequently see but don't talk to two women in their thirties who are twins. They always dress identically and have been part of my visual life for at least fifteen years. Once in a while, they get front-paged—or call it "pair creation," so I am sure you've seen them, especially those of you who live in England. They were on the BBC TV programme called Odd Box. These passengers are with us now—I'd ask them to stand up but that might be rude given the current context.

Let me tell you about our research, our tube research. The train emerges in a mortuary green-tiled subway stop, Dufferin. I leave the train at the middle of the station. Imran, or was it Anver, takes the photos, and in a few minutes he'll meet me at Spadina on the west platform. No flash. The trains are noisy. One never hears or feels this in Montreal. In Toronto, it's steel wheels on steel rails, and steel gripping asbestos to make the train stop. I exit to inspect Dufferin Street, which shakes beneath my feet as the trains writhe under the city like Islamic cobras who have immigrated from Parassinikkadavu Snake Park in India.

All this diary talk of trains, snakes, and twins has made me and Anver fall into a collective sleep like the two Sikhs I saw at an airport lounge. After a few minutes, I wake up and I start daydreaming of Rabi' al-thani. Anver is still sleeping. I walk down the hall and notice a new woman with sagging jowls sitting in a large red leather armchair. She is wearing pink fishnet stockings. The river is visible from her chair. Refusing to die, she will issue silence for one entire decade. She looks out at the ducks on the ice. Her name is Tatjana. I find her silence resonant, abundant. We make eye contact until an old man—Ralph Das, ex-journalist—shuffles into the small kitchen. There are brown coffee rings and toast crumbs on the counter. He looks into the living room and shouts the word "messy" into the huddle of card players. They collectively turn around and then go back to the card game. Undistractable, the lot.

Linda, wearing a red dress, walks to the kitchen and looks back at me. I move to another location beside a window. I'm being a gentle and sensitive old-age presence. Minding my own business "far from the madding crowd," and far from the memory tests. Monday, 14:30, elevator upstairs, Dr. Jefferies, neuropathologist, age eighteen—thinks she knows more than me—will perform tests to see if I have teratomas of the hippocampus and if all the terrorist genetic switches are turned off: or on, or both, at the same time. How many numbers can I remember? Name the last five addresses I lived in? How many fingers do I have? Her games continue.

> *In March of a certain year, terrorists—that's what they call them when they don't look in the mirror—bombed a European target. The target was not London Bridge. The explosion changed the outcome of the national elections, causing this particular nation to pull their troops out of somewhere where the locals are influenced by only one book, and this book is not the Philosophiae Naturalis Principia Mathematica. When a mass accelerates in a million different directions along with a colourful, high-definition flash, some smoke and some bent*

train rails, European and North American mores—call it voting patterns—change at a rate inversely proportional to the distance travelled by a patriot to become a terrorist.

The rate of change of European morals is inversely proportional to the summation of the distance travelled by a patriot towards freedom and liberation. As imperial plunder and tactics become desperate, and the distance to liberation is nearer, the need for violence is inevitably multiplied. If the imperialist walks away, the scope of splattering is smaller. Therefore, (dy/dx) of European Morals = Σ (1/(imperialism-Liberation).

The sub and superscript on the summation sign, will have i = 0 terror at the bottom,

y = full scale terror on top:

dy

- x = plunder

dx (European morals) = Σ (imperialism freedom)

c = freedom

But in the end, all one needs to make the imperialists listen is:

F = MA + bang + to whatever the spin over the square root of Israelis and their corollaries. This is a slightly more perfected expression:

$$\frac{dy}{dx} = \sum_{i=0}^{i=fst} \frac{1}{(I(y)-c(y))} \qquad \frac{dy}{dx} = \frac{1}{\sum_{i=0}^{i=fst} (I_i(y)-c_i(y))}$$

6

Blue blankets, Russell Square

In the corner, on the red chair, still watching the river, Usha receives another call. She utters soft words into her cell phone. It rings again shortly afterwards. Doctor calling to make an appointment? I turn off the radio and detach the alligator clip from the antenna; in the era of the web I listen to my shortwave for fun. An incoherent mixture of two or more European languages comes out in a gush: German predominates. Linda sees me place the radio on the shiny wood table beside the sofa. I will not forget it there. I take memory pills.

As night falls, the river looks like flowing pewter. Bright spotlights trailing along the water's edge, igniting the grass making yellow-green patches. The ice on the blue river moves more slowly than usual. A spiral of mist rolls off the pond into the pointy hats of the nearby evergreens. The evening is a marker: change of clothes, the home winds down. The asthmatics get a hit of oxygen before they sleep.

Iqbal Masoume, who lives here, is a friend in the operational sense. Yet he, like a few of the others, keeps to himself in a room at one end of a light-filled hall. I am in his room with him. He is not as close to me as Anver. He never seems unhappy, enjoys listening to the news every day. A few remember that he was the brains behind a famous bombing. Free publicity, provided you don't kill me; that, I'm afraid, would be the ultimate publicity, he tells his friends here. We won't kill you, we all assure him. Besides, Iqbal, who can find you here? Rotting mind. Buried in snow, in Canada, in the province of Quebec. Who would look here? Don't worry. More important urban centres are suspected. I'd play that seven of hearts now if I were you.

Iqbal had gone missing, somewhere, years ago. But he's here with us now. He didn't come across on that boat with us. They say he did something wrong. Who are they? Intelligence? Pig-eaters the lot. Now, he's fine and tucked into bed like a rag doll under the pink blankets. Blue blankets were used to cover the dead at Russell Square underground. In this century, we have foil heat blankets, much lighter than the blankets and duvets of the last century. I say goodbye and tenderly walk out of his room.

And a few minutes pass. Anver shuffles into my room. He sits. He has new running shoes on. He's fit. So is his mind. He asks me why I mentioned class and class origins in the last bit?

"I didn't mention it and I am not mentioning it. I think you might have made a mistake in hearing. Is this possible?" We hear an old train whistle.

7

Bereavement support group

Is Jean an old operative we used for interconnections? He's patently too young. Must still be day one of the pill. I can describe how the pill works. I wake up. I go to the doctor, who, in Wolof, asks me to roll up my sleeve. He gives me a shot of a transparent cobalt blue liquid. I look at him through the large, squat syringe. He looks dark black until a cloud of my blood back-spirals into the syringe. But why call it a pill if it's a shot in the arm? No, that shot in the arm is for some piss or shit test. Dr. Babrika Fall doesn't give me the pills. No, I take them myself every day, and here's the procedure: I open my night table draw; I open the container; I take the pill with a glass of non-African water; I close and replace the container in the drawer. Then, a few weeks later, another doctor comes to my room to say that I now have to stop for wee bits. Almost at once, the walls fall and become electrum which I make into earrings. Disclarity. Which I also enjoy. Two weeks on, two weeks off. *The New England Journal of Medicine* is my patron saint.

Finally, it's summer. The entire home population is out on the lawn of blurring memories. Old fathers and mothers who can't remember the faces of sons and daughters are all there under the unifying sunshine waiting for the inheritance jackpot. When will they next visit—the sons or daughters, that is? Why did this or that one's son or daughter visit and not mine? Ragged memories of divorces, separations, lawyers.

In the small reading room of the home, I walk over to aged Tatjana. I ask: "Do you have your boarding pass?" She's tall, majestic, and introduces me to her daughter, who is shorter. She's surrounded by her tall sons, dressed in colourful Hawaiian shirts. Her daughter bids me a tactical welcome. The welcome is not about being nice to me: I'm an old fart but I've a reputation for being stimulating. The daughter probably thinks that if her mother has a male friend here, then she will feel less obligated to visit. It takes so much time to visit dying parents. Why can't guilty sons and daughters see that I can see what they're thinking? After chatting, I visit another table in the room.

A home picnic with cucumber sandwiches and sunshine is taking place outside. After a while, Tatjana and I walk together, leaving the groupings of old people on the green grass. She touches my hand. The daughter notices. The picnic continues.

Everyone turns around. Suddenly, a broken bladder pops out of a body heading skyward. It spirals out of control, spurting out a slow trickle of warm piss on wrinkled faces, shiny overpriced computer-driven wheelchairs, diluting the tea. Usha starts singing "Yellow Submarine." I hold out an umbrella over Tatjana.

Push a button and the chip on the wheelchair memorizes a certain path to the doctor, to the lawn, to the swimming pool, to the Bereavement Support Group in which we'd hear conversation like this: We'd never discussed his last wishes. Suddenly I had only a few hours to choose a funeral home and make plans that would affect my entire family. The lesson has been well learned. After this experience, I decided to plan my own funeral, right down to the smallest detail. It was actually comforting. I did it mostly for my kids—I don't want them to have to go through that again. But I also did it for myself. I thought I didn't have any kids.

The lawn is filled with leaky piss-bitterness memories of the husband who beat you; the kidney that failed you; the liver you resent; the DNA that unravels more quickly than it ought; the memory of a wife who left you for another man (maybe your best friend); the partner in a law firm who fucked you on the desk on May Day; the man who got you out of the firm so you have to work for The City at a thousandth of what you've earned with the more corrupt firm, which you loved, which you and only you got off the ground. Head offices in New York and Bangkok. Filthy employees, behind your back, they say that Jews and Chinks are running the entire show. Blurred short-termish memories of who is winning the current game of lawn bowling, or when the game began, or what happened before or after lunch, or what one had for lunch, dinner, or what dinner or lunch is, or if one has become a cannibal.

Jeff is the winner at lawn bowling, august, round-faced Jeff. He's intelligent, but the lawn balls have more memory retention. He wins at lawn balls, but in a way the balls win. He wears a white T-shirt with a few food stains on it. Every time I see him, I make a point of asking him what his son's name is. He pretends to be hard of hearing. I repeat the question. Nurse Linda gently takes me aside and suggests that I stop asking him this particular question. She saw him crying in his room while looking for his son's name in his address book. I think I'm doing him a favour by asking him, I say. "No, you're not doing him any favours, he just can't remember his son's name. Just chat with him about other things." When the nurse goes away, I repeat the question: "So how's your son, what's his name? Coming for your birthday, is he?" No nurse is going to stop me from asking what I want to ask. "Can't remember" means that he ought to go on the memory pills.

Geriatric skin so elastic that it could be used for slingshots. Just cut some off from the neck and use it. If I had a son I'd remember what his name is, I tell long tall Jeff with black balls in both hands. Expensive shoes Jeff wears.

Linda approaches my table, which I am sharing with Tatjana's family with Hawaiian-shirted sons. Tatjana is watching a black ball roll down memory lane: she slowly turns around to look at me. Horn-rimmed glasses. Smiles again. A black ball rolls and rolls. There's an old Irish woman who forgets things—events very quickly: by the time the ball touches another ball, she has forgotten why she was looking at me. Also, she may have forgotten what the round object is called or what its function is. Clunk. Ah! Ball. But she smiles, yet another smile.

The ball is black. The grass is green. She has periods in which her memory functions with average long-term and better than average short-term. Today is not a good day for long or short-term memory—her memory is bringing into view an image of a Kellogg's Corn Flakes box from 1950. She tells me that her daughter is visiting. She has given her some perfume, which smells of something she can't remember. "Perhaps," she says, "I can remember—perhaps it smells like a perfume caught between two things: the corn flakes in the box and a saucer of fresh dill which has been cooling in the fridge? My memory is good, and getting better. It's hard to recall the names of smells. I remember you." She looks at me. "You—John Macleod can sing Zeera Lynn's 'We'll Meet Again'. You sang it when we ate at McDonalds."

Who has more memory, the black ball or the man turning toward me after having sent it down the lawn? I'd say the ball. A woman who looks as though she could be called Beulah replies: "Green." But dark or light green?

What makes Beulah more appealing than the ones without memories is that she can remember—memory and remembering are two different things. Memory is an object, remembering is a process, I suggest. His head—which may not be filled with intelligence—is filled with precision when it comes to remembering what he had for breakfast, lunch, dinner and what colour socks he put on this morning—blue on the left, olive green on the right. Old people here have the-putting-on-the-different-socks disease. The memory pills change all that: red on the right, red on the left; navy on the right, navy on the left ad nauseam.

Memory: the final commodity. I can never underestimate the pleasure of talking with a person with a good memory. Beulah, former teacher of history rambles out the following dates: 1688, 1759, 1492, 711, 1947, 1945, 1871, 1215, 711, 1789, 1917, 1648, 1066. What happened in 711, I ask? "Magna Carta," she says.

The Man-who-looks-like-a-police-detective-but-isn't-or-is-Anver, Linda, the doctor, the cook, all have memory. No money, nor real brains, but they remember details. This is what we agers all are jealous of. We have money, that much we remember, but we can't remember the memories. So what good is money? All you remember is that you have it.

The conversation concludes. The Man-who-looks-like-a-police-detective-but-isn't-or-is-Anver comes back another day. I ask him the name of his son.

Tatjana Lucrece nears my table as Anver leaves. I say good bye to him without introducing him to Tatjana. I'm a few natural numbers away from eighty-five. Eyes sharp as a hawk's, more memory, and other possibilities.

8

Perfidious Albion

There's an old Irish woman here with Homeric storytelling skills and who is as innocent as an underground tube stop in London. Her name is Usha, she has light blue eyes. She immigrated to Canada many moons ago because she wanted to live in a classless society. Bloody Sunday for some has become a faded memory; she had grown up in a working-class neighbourhood where English soldiers walk. Her stories pull me in: I sit with her and while away the hours in a room where the walls are painted a light blue. She sits in such a way that I can see the fertilized green lawn behind her. I am the only one in this house who knows and understands her stories: Perfidious Albion meets a humble representative of Mohammad (PBUH).

Usha has lovely upright shoulders, which are usually covered with white cotton shirts. She has luminous white hair, and she wears stockings of different colours—I mean left leg one colour, right leg another. We take our exercise together—walks in the woods surrounding the home. Occasionally, when I have supper with her I see how she cuts the food on her plate. She composes a colourful morsel of food on a fork, which she uses in an un-American way—inverted. The fork methodically migrates around the plate, picking up a bit of pale green overcooked asparagus, amalgamating it with a bit of shepherd's pie; all this touches a bit of gravy on the northern part of the plate before rising into her mouth, where false teeth slowly masticate the food. She smiles at me when the morsel has gone down. "The afternoon whisks by, doesn't it Joseph," she says. This gravely touches me. "Gravely"—nice word for geezers to be using. I've fallen in love with her. And I'll tell Linda all about it. We are in love. I think I'll settle down now. With her. Beside the river. Her old hands touch me, her arms move around my waist when we stroll on the grounds when everyone in Pierrefonds is sleeping. We know this is the end, and it'll be a whimper, a sleep that never ends, so there is an intensity to our glances. You see, without being overly dramatic—she's trying a new drug—Guinea pig-Usha, that brings back memories—that final commodity that only us rich can afford. Besides, what do they have to remember? Chef Boyardee? Cigarettes and warm milk? And, fuck their memories.

Late at night, as I make my way to Usha's room, I walk past Iqbal's. I see him lying on his bed, looking out the window. Sometimes I knock, walk in and chat with him. Tonight, I ask him if he really had been the brains behind it all. Or was it me? Where are you now, I ask him—in that high-rise where we once met or are you here with me in this home? I'm here, he'd say, ultra-rationalist, no memory loss for him. Yes, I know you grew up in London near Hampstead Heath among the starlings.

Having tucked him in, I walk toward the cold window. Three airplanes in the night sky are lining up for landing. I think about Usha before I head in the direction of her room. I remember the broadcast of many years ago. Or was it the voice in the airport? 13:00 hours Greenwich Mean Time. Iqbal Masoume, please come to the information desk. A few passengers from Jeddah, Teheran, Islamabad and Detroit want to ask you a few questions about your blank blank relationship with blank blank. I decide not to visit Usha tonight.

The upside-down opaque bowl on the ceiling of my room beside the river houses a security camera which sees all the time. A kind of Allah of the modern age. Not all the residents have a room camera. The nurses can watch me, in case something happens. I try to look into the eye of the security camera—but there is only an infantile, shiny black bowl with an evenly coloured surface: dead personified.

Moonlight falls on our purgatory. The slow river sags into a pond, making a mirror filled with stars. Most geezers have 20:20 vision if they want, and most want, but only rich old bastards like us can. A friend was telling me that he has a poor friend who is old and needs money for an operation. Only the rich can see.

Reflected in the river-pond, I can see nearby Alpha Centauri in the dotted, fast-flowing cosmological clock which can't stop but can only change speeds and times, just as the Jew predicted. Another century whisks by, reptiles become things with two feet, lungs *and* feathers. Morning birds chirp outside my window. My legs are tired; this explains why I am from time to time inhabiting a luxury wheelchair which glides along, wheels not touching the ground. I can walk, I am just playing with someone else's wheelchair. The off-white hall is graced with twenty-first century versions of French-Canadian impressionist paintings. The painkillers make the French-Canadian landscape paintings an Abstract Expressionist blur, and almost tolerable as art. But when I slow down I can see the ugly paintings for what they are. "Why am I moving like this?" I ask my wheelchair pusher. "Why does life become a stream of questions? What sort of tests does he want to do? Why do all questions become useless? Why does intellectual laziness set in in old age?"

Nurse Linda has long hands that move me. Something moves inside me when I see her orientalist half-moons. Her touch is hushed, kind, her conversation's never filled with idiocies, banalities, misconceived star clusters. Unique nurse. When we get to the long smooth hall, we take the elevator up two floors. "Nothing complicated," she assures me.

"Am I flirting with you again? Trying to get into your pants at seventy-something makes me feel good."

"Intimate language today, my, my. How are you getting along with Tatjana? Have you met her daughter?" I hear the not so subtle ding of the elevator door at the same time I notice a fallen pine cone in a snowscape in one of the revolutionary French-Canadian paintings of evergreens. "The dead banker's wife's daughter moves with the movements and the sounds of old age," I say.

"The daughter is no more than fifty-something."

"Numerically young. Linda are you going to leave me after giving me my four o'clock pills?" We surface on another floor. I add: "Notice how I'm not nosy. I can stay with you until six this evening, or should I say that I want to stay with you until six this evening.

Here I'm sitting in a chair. I look out of the window. In regular rhythmic movements, fine snow moves past. My favourite nurse is in the room. She sees my theatrical stare. "What is it about me that you find ..." She moves with finesse and directness. "I know you were accused of something very bad—this is what you keep telling me, isn't it? Was it murder?" she asks, then stops to look at my wheelchair and continues: "What about all those silly radio programmes you listen to on your computer with your friends here? We've never had a group of old people here before, most are individually here—I mean they are not family like you all seem to be. How did you all end up in the same old folk's home together?"

I say: "I didn't do anything wrong. We're all old friends —commune friends. Codswollop. Thrown out of court ... no proof. Proof, that wonderful toy of western democracy. Bunch of cunts. Never even went to court—except in my diary."

Linda responds: "Oh, you're angry. I know you're innocent. But you did arrange it all, didn't you? So are you really innocent?"

"You have to use that word *arrange*, I notice."

"Thrown out of court ... no proof. Proof, that wonderful toy of western democracy. Evidence. Make me repeat myself why don't you? Never went to court. All fantasy."

"I know you're innocent," she concedes.

"You see you're falling in love with me. Yes, I arranged it all, but, or should I say and I'm innocent."

"What are the details?"

9

Haeinsa Codex

I open my computer, which is as small as a popsicle stick. The keyboard—still with us—is all H-graphic: so is the screen, which I can make as large as a house but if I make it too large, others can read my diary—usually of a very personal nature—and the image-text resolution is not impressive. Even if I were to project my screen on a cloud or on a fog patch in the sky or at 8000 metres or on the home lawn, I could still read it super clearly with a telescope. And they are not even called computers any more. My codex—that is what computers are now called—is a super-fast model made in the UK (United Korea): the Haeinsa Codex comes with time-licensed software called 0-47. These things still have hardware—all you do is rub the stick once and the codex appears like a movie before your eyes. Same thing happens when you rub a bunch of foreskins—they expand into a suitcase. The codex is about the size of a book, an early edition of *The Wealth of Nations*.

There is a section of my voice diary I call British Hairs. I've set it to voice a similar accent and I've set the background sound to nineteenth century train sounds with a whistle here and there. Nobody is around, except Anver. All alone in the cosmos with my popsicle stick.

Here's my past life of action with some still and some real time pictures—all projected on my white towel, pinned on the wall in my room. My current life is also one of action—but the action doesn't require passports and old-fashioned boarding passes, and standing in line-ups to move through the elephant trunks. Whenever I've moved with passport in hand through the tube that takes you to the aircraft, I've looked at the walls of the trunk, which are light grey. I've felt this tube contract and expand, undulate with a thin mucus film that ushers in the passengers. There is a miasma of hydrogen sulphide and coca. British Hairways.

> *Montreal trains emerge in vast, spacious stops, sometimes surrounded by three-storey high coloured panes of glass decorated by feminist artists. The station names always appear in smaller-than-European station font cut into ceramic tiles: Bonaventure, Champ-de-Mars, Square-Victoria. In the late afternoon, the Outremont metro stop fills with Russian teenagers smoking and necking with other Russian kids. The overweight white and black kids watch the Russians in tight jeans. As young Moslems, we enjoyed this metro scene, but, unfortunately, our religion prevents us from copping a feel in public.*

Anver laughs—that isn't what they say in Cairo. I stop the diary and wait for him to stop laughing.

"Anver, you finished?"

"I've finished. All this for a deathbed confession?"

Montreal's metro trains run on rubber wheels; their departure from the stations creates a Doppler sound effect. I keep imagining a musician from the Montreal Symphony Orchestra sitting among the passengers while playing one single note on a French horn. Passengers get off the Sherbrooke metro station into a minus 40 Celsius morning. More harmonic departures. We prefer morning rush hours. We prefer the Doppler trigger, but some like to judge when the train has hit full speed. Here in Anglo-Asian Toronto we are part of an underground system where steel on steel is the rule. This French-Canadian city—Montreal—has the most spacious and cheapest metro system in the world, tickets cost $3.00. This is a world record, take it from Immy and me. I think Anver came too but I am not sure. Also, Immy thinks this is the best Metro in the world. However, the thinner gauge might require another kind of rucksack—er—knapsack due to the passenger density and train velocity. And we'd time it so it would go off at the end of the French horn Doppler effect, when the train has reached full speed. If we hit between 06:00 and 07:45, we splatter the dark immigrants. The white passengers use the Metro after 08:12. A fact not worth overlooking. We made calculations that the

Islamic radius of destruction is the greatest at the fastest speed, but the blast trail elongates, spreading innards along the Judeo-Christian tunnel walls.

The radius islamicus is the farthest distance a camel part is thrown from the blast centre. I mentioned doing state vectors, but our supervising Mullah didn't understand anything beyond first year cal.

The ultimate fantasy for a knapper is to be on a mis-railed train accidently heading toward a telescopic collision with another train hitting peak speed at Westminster. But our ultimate fantasy is now OT—orbital terrorism.

Anver touches the stop button on the computer and asks: "Why didn't we ... why didn't we do that? Why? It would have been so much more fun than riding all those underground trains. We could have gone to space."

I restart the reading by touching the computer, saying: "Anver, we would not have gone to outer space. We would have launched the thing to hit the International Space Station and other orbital targets. All we needed to do is to buy a few rockets—that can do the escape velocity thing—from our chink friends and bob's your cha-cha. But I digress ..."

In Montreal, on the Orange Line, during Ramadan, a young Arab reads a mini Koran about six inches from his nose. Immy and I almost approach him, but he could be a plant. We find it pretentious that this provincial hick, most likely from Libya, would read the Holy book in front of kaffers who have tons of make-up on. We don't mind make-up. We notice that his eyes detach from the holy Koran when the metro stop Plamondon is scraped into our ears. Robotically, the good book goes into his pocket, and he steps beyond the sliding doors onto the next stop, which is Namur. The dark orange ceramic tiles cover the entire station. From there, Ali-watch-me-as-I-read-the-holy-book-on-the-train catches a bus; to where, one wonders. We're not going to knap in the early morning because there are too many non-whites. After 08:12 the white nine-to-fivers waltz in.

Someone in the home is playing the *Blue Danube* by Johann Strauss II, composed in 1866 according to the World Narrow Web. Did I just use the word waltz in my diary? This level of synchronicity plagues my life—there is one connection after another.

Somehow, Mirza Marlow, also known as Mr. Kutta Kunjar, an ex-Czech helper, got us advanced plastic, which is light as Kleenex. And, these days, you can see through it, and it smells like Munich on that inspirational Tuesday.

Toronto subway stations are sombre-toned in relation to Montreal's uplifting metro stations, and therefore automatically deserve sui-knapsack. The Toronto subway system has announcements in a bucolic English transmitted via broken-sounding speaker cones. The Old Mill stop is surrounded by glass, making the enigma of arrival like gliding into a sodium light-filled station, surrounded by a view of a deep inner-city valley filled with green trees —Toronto is indeed Canada's model city. But nothing in the world beats an arrival in a Montreal metro stop.

Toronto's subway names are English. Islington is followed by Kipling followed by more meat-and-potato names such as Warden and Keele. The Wardenites and Keeleists lead to High Park which takes us to thunderous heights: Runnymede, where, in 1215 rebellious barons imposed the Magna Carta on Toronto. This TTC stop symbolizes the roots of modern western democracy. Today, the spirit of the Magna Carta has converted into an Uzi aimed at heads of Palestinians.

Anver leaves for a few minutes to water his elephant and then walks back into my room. He looks at the screen near my lap and points to his ears with both hands. I wind back a few seconds so he can catch up.

He sits and listens, making no comments.

The Toronto subway system is not a sealed underground; trains occasionally ride on surface tracks, letting the sunlight burst into moving trains. Torontonians, who are mainly from China and other countries where Caucasians don't come from—watch the condos-for-sale blur past Lake Ontario as the sunset sets. We have to consider these east-west Bloor trains which start off underground but also surface like mammals. These trains offer excellent media. I mean we could have a blast just as the train comes out of a tunnel into the sunlight, couldn't we? This is what we did. This augmented the sunshine after the darkness of the tunnel.

And, because we are sympathetic to the working-class crew of South Asians who have to clean up the mess—in fact our mess—we have decided to calculate a double eastbound-westbound knapblast—that is, explicitly: have both trains popped simultaneously in the same area where the trains surface. This way the entire city will not be paralyzed and we will not be hated by every single neighbourhood in Toronto. I admit that when we do things indiscriminately we get hated by all the neighbourhoods in any particular city. We don't want to be disliked city-wide. Surface blast areas are also cleaned up more quickly than tunnel events. We would like the city to get back to normal as soon as possible. We have decided to have the double pop-pop take place within seven minutes' ambulance ride to a very nearby hospital. Seven minutes? How do we know? We timed it: three ambulance trials. Our partners in these operations phone ambulances a few minutes before the actual event so as to keep causalities within reason. Of course, we'd like to give hours and hours of notice to the hospital to get ready for more beds, but if we gave hours and hours of notice we'd lose the other effects that we need to get on with. We pre-warn the ambulances: we do this to prove that we're not cold-blooded terrorists. We're green-minded, book-loving types who are aiming for some sort of balance. When was the last time you heard of troops from a white country informing the local hospitals that something was coming down the line?

We continually inform the hospitals, the ambulances, and then, lastly, the media. Keeping the hospitals and nurses' unions in the loop reduces suffering. And surface bombings require maximum speed for TV. Some of our partners have said that nothing beats a banged-up tunnel for pressing the flesh and winning elections by using Islam. We thought about conducting internal tunnel jobs but our Christian side got the better of us: in our filthy homelands, many of us went to private Christian schools. Of course, we even thought about end-to-end station pops—at Kennedy and at the other far end of the line at

> *Kipling with a triangulated bang at Dundas, and a two-knapsack bang for the Magnacarta-ites at the Runnymede stop. And even one innocent little bang on Ward's Island—about a fifteen minute ferry ride from the Toronto Ferry Docks at the foot of Bay Street and Queens Quay. But that Toronto Islands stuff got nixed by us not our leadership. We simply do not want to be hated by every neighbourhood in Toronto. We successfully created a dot-to-dot star of David with our mathematically organized bombing of locations across the Greater Toronto Area, but usually we've been selective and operate only on one part of the city. Long ago, we gave up being monkey-see-monkey-do and causing all that flamboyant global impact. None of us committed suicide, that was a myth. We planned. We placed. We left. We saw it on TV. We went to the next city, all in search of balance. We played tennis with cousins and nieces, we ate ham sandwiches with mayonnaise and mint. We didn't do hematidrosis in the Garden of Gethsemane.*

Anver responds to the voiced diary notes on our possible past. "But you're making it up as you go along. We did a triangle pop pop pop in Toronto during the eighties. You're forgetting and you're dry-cleaning our past."

"Dry-cleaning? What do you mean dry-cleaning our past?"

"I am having fun listening to your doctoring of what happened."

> *The real trick is to get all three at peak acceleration, Herr Doppler tighter and tighter frequencies hissing to high heaven. A chap called Javid Goonda Atta, who studied Penrose tiles, gave us two timings: we should be stepping on the train just before the driver sticks his head out to see if all is clear for departure. Catch the train closest to 08:27. We practice many times and compare the timings. Say goodbye as you hit peak speed. Say goodbye? But none of us became chutney with the bang. We placed. We got off at the next stop. The Runnymede rucksack should leave as close to 08:13. Setting off the device at peak speed is important. It's pointless and boring to hit during deceleration or when one is stationary. After the 08:13s have happened, they will shut down the subway, but not before 08:13. We dump our jackets before we get on the actual train so we are just in Elvis T-shirts. The Toronto Transit Commission (TTC) might wait until 08:31 to close the entire system. A Sussex dropout, yet Trent university graduate, Sabe Zameenpargira, gave us all the numbers. The TTC will know by 08:13 that there is no absolute innocence, only degrees of innocence. Entangled innocence if*

you add the human tissues that are liberated during the blast.

Russell Square ... Piccadilly Line, Heathrow Terminal H, Air Canada to Pearson International Airport, switch to TTC bus, board the Bloor line at Kipling; twenty minutes to pick up the knapsack at Islington, to be left on the train at Dundas West, or if one were feeling like it, not to leave—ha, that is what the journalists think. Perhaps we'll hit Anchorage or an iceberg. Anver asks: "John, what's the point of hitting an iceberg? Sure, of course, I understand the berg part of the operation but what's the point? The thing will just turn to water. You want to kill them with flooding?"

Many wonderful and funny things happened during our training. Many in the outside world thought we didn't have any ideology behind us except Islam.

We did more than ten physicalist operations with the Filipino communists under their command but under the firm mental influence of LTM (Lahore Teaching Madrassa). CNN liked to portray it all as Islamic doom, Purda, Islamic boom, Islamic gloom and blood blooming rancid honour killings of our daughters because they took white sperm in the mouth in the school yard, destroying Flintstone-y idolatry-loaded statues of Buddhas at Bamiyan, slitting sheep throats, right before Christmas, and right in the middle of Edgeware Road—

this is all far from the truth. We have communist sympathies, but we couldn't blend Mao into Mohammad (PBUH); we couldn't polycreate Maohammad. Mao was far too rational, reasonable and systematic for us. Too many five-year plans and sequential commitments. And non-Islamic chinks are without poetry. With Islamic goofs we, at least, had some poetry. And any Fanonist will understand why our colleagues in Afghanistan had to blast away the Buddhists in stone. Save them for some slanty-eyed Jap-Chinks to photograph? To photograph stones while the locals don't have much at all: there has to be a limit.

The food that the communists ate in the Philippines didn't impress us at all but that's not the point. We went to help them with the hope of bringing capitalism to its knees, not to have a nice evening daavat beside a blue river. Admittedly, we did place the bang machine.

Yes. Yes, we wanted to hit innocent upper-class types. The commie intellectuals didn't want to splatter the rich, rather they wanted to build consensus across all vegetarian groups and actually not hurt nor want to hurt the ruling class oppressors. Obviously, we had difficulty with their attitude, but we never resisted or caused any leadership problems due to this disagreement. We did what they wanted. We knew some maths and engineering that would go into their particular kinds of needs. They were less educated but had a vision and weren't benumbed by a vast spectrum of capitalist responses to resistance.

We didn't have a Sri Lankan bang signature because we simply didn't have the quantity. Lankan bangs were super-loaded with Soviet stuff. I like super-loaded jobs. If those chaps needed two units of bang to do a one unit operation, they would use fifteen or twenty bang units just to impress the followers with what a splendiferous job they could do. The amount they used would literally cut a 747 clean in two, one side flying off to Calgary, the other to Philadelphia. We Islamics were impressed but thought that 20 units was too showoffy, which is not permitted (PBUH). We mentioned these details to a Filipina commander —and yes, they were mostly women—who was not impressed, but found us perfectly reliable.

No one's saying that the end results were funny. Except to us. When we'd get the visuals + sound afterward from our almost-Chinawoman-camerawoman, Anver would laugh at some upper-middle-class label-wearing rich bitch howling in pain just because her leg was 1432 centimetres from the rest of her, and her new $400 jeans were ruined. Where's my leg? What happened to my shopping trip? Where's my driver? My shoes need a stain-remover. Why does my hair look tousled? Anver would say something like:

look, we accidently blew the kaffer's leg off and there is a city of blood coming from the ruptured arteries. Khoonsher. Tisk tisk. The communists would not laugh at all. They just "analyzed" the footage thinking of how they could produce fewer not more injuries. Here, Maoism seemed irrational to us. We just kept quiet when they went into serious aftermath mode. Why go through all the calculations, staking, and planting when the results could not be treated as fun? At LTM we were taught not only chemistry but also how to have fun learning new things. Nobody used suicide bangs. The western world does have a good hearty Christian laugh when they pop us, and yes we had laughs also.

Kala Mukudma, a fellow student from West Yorkshire, now with us at the Lahore Terrorist Madrassa, pondered: "Suicide bombings are good for the circulation of the blood, good too for high cholesterol, a solution for root-canal work, haemorrhoids, anal fissures, bladder cancer and lower back pain—all could now be solved in a flash. But how do we get, or rather make a product that would get rid of back pain pronto, and to put it all on TV? I mean it couldn't be a pill or a computer programme—it would have to be something you'd eat on a regular basis like Kellogg's Buds with psyllium, something you could advertise. I say I have a massive toothache. The only way out is to remove myself—but should I remove myself with Islamo-toothpaste? Why not take a few corrupt cunt politicians also? I mean, like fuck 'em." Safade Jamun Samoondar, my dear Safade, has a Scottish accent when he speaks Punjabi. He made good Pushto which is a way of cooking lamb in Sumarkand. And the bit about getting virgins in paradise is pure CNN Israeli horseshit. What about the Japanese during world war two? Does anyone ask them if they were offered environmentally friendly Toyotas in the afterlife?

Anyway, we're thinking of calculating the Moscow Metro due to their actions in Pomegranate Land, but Dimitri said not to even think about it—he told us that Mohammad would not like us anymore if we even once thought about it. And besides, we were having a time pronouncing names such as: Sokolnicheskaya, Tagansko-Krasnopresnenskaya, and Serpukhovsko-Timiryazevskaya. Therefore, we went without telling Mohammad: we went, we saw, we didn't knap. Lucky Russians, unlucky Chechens.

I said, you should stop making jokes about such serious radii. Javid Chambers, a member of our headless group, replied: "Mullah X said wear your education lightly—why use the plural for radius when you don't really have to?"

We leave downtown Toronto, Union Station

a little after sunset. We have surfaced into a treeless Christian suburb where many Chinese Buddhists live. The Chinese always vote for the extreme right. We'll fix them like we fixed the Spaniards who, after the European bombing, voted for a left-wing homosexual who brought the Spanish troops home from Pomegranate Land.

There are so many of us in Toronto, we'd blend in. And before the hicks could say diddly squat, we'd be back in Brick Lane eating suicide kebabs. The CCTV ratio between London and Toronto is 34:1. Surveillance makes us smarter.

The Montreal metro cars are light blue with grey seats, much narrower than the wide-bodied trains in Toronto. We found the names pleasant to our ears but the Arabs who worked with us didn't. For fun, we'd call our Arab colleagues A-rabs; they'd laugh when we'd say that A-rabs are as naive as sardines.

Mont Royal, Sherbooke, Berri-UQAM, Camp-de-Mars, Place-D'Armes, Square-Victoria, Bonaventure, Lucien-L'Allier, George Vanier, and Lionel-Groulx (who was a deep jew-hater). These goofy French-Canadians actually named a stop after a Nazi sympathizer: Lionel-Groulx. Groulx was an aunty-Semite. We are not anti-Semitic. We are pro-Semitic-Semtex. These names aren't worth bombing. We sent Israelipegs to Mullah X-37 in Lahore via three Hotmail accounts; he sent them on to Mullah Ghandmukin in Waziristan: no dice. He didn't think that Montreal was worth it. Actually, we didn't have to send the jpegs. We had a messenger tell him the usernames and passwords and all he did was check our draft box.

But in mysterious ways the British army helped us all along. We knew we had a counter-mole in our group—he must have told them, but they let it all happen. Admittedly, it is a baroque theory but there you have it. This is the reason why the British didn't do any autopsies on the bodies—they knew that they would find U.K. home office explosive traces, placed right there by Mrs. El Moneypenny.

Mullah X37—a graduate of both Saint Martin's and The School of Wog Studies in Bloomsbury—thought the photos weren't detailed enough. He did, however, say that Islamic activists who are imprisoned in western jails or in the prisons of Arab uncle toms are literally gold in the Bank of Allah. That they are in prison makes our hearts beat and make us bomb those towering glass cities.

An Oriental woman with high heels is sitting beside me; she's reading the same article in The National Post as I am. It's about Louis Farrakhan, the Nation of Islam leader who is flamboyant and talks in racist riddles about Jews. She notices me noticing her; we both look up and smile. I ask her about the names of the subway stops. She says: "Well they don't reflect Toronto anymore."

"Why?" I ask. She replies: "Our tax money should reflect the new Canada not the Canada of Bathurst, Saint Patrick, College, Wellesley, Cunt's Park."

I must have mis-heard what she said, but I leave nothing to the imagination.

"What names do you want to see?" I ask.

"Chun Lai should replace Eglinton. We pay taxes. The city should reflect us. And if they don't change the names, then I agree with your bombing project of Toronto's Subway."

Well that 905 chink was very supportive, most of them just think about money, and they never inter-marry with A-rabs, who they claim always want to conduct sodomy—just ask the girls in Tokyo or Shanghai. A-rab boyfriend means no pregnancies.

Two homosexuals get on at Coxwell: therefore, Carlton should be renamed Yasser Arafat. Kennedy should be renamed or co-named, Fidel Castro to make the Canadians of Cuban origin feel nicely integrated—just like in Miami. On the north-south line, the colourless North York Centre should blur into Sparrow to keep Black Canadians integrated despite their patties. St. Clair West becomes Tintoretto. St. Andrew should be sandblasted off for Indira Gandhi. Names like Elephant and Castle or Seven Sisters are so strange even to us who were born here, that we feel, well, we don't know what we feel.

Poetic sounding names, such as Elephant and Castle, Shepherd's Bush, Seven Sisters should not be changed for South Asian poets such as Mirza Galib or Faiz Ahamd Faiz because they are good the way they are—the South Asian Lesbians Association of Toronto of course wants to rename the subway stops after Bengali sisters. I am sure not even a cheap copycat knapper would knapsack stops with Moslem names. Imagine Javid Chambers or Anver Ahmad knapping a metro stop with a name such as Hussain Hussaine. The current Prime Minister is thinking of changing Russell Square to Mohammad Ali Jinnah just for this reason. It's the only choice he has. We didn't like the sound of Victoria, Vauxhall, Arsenal, Russell Square, Oval and White City; so here are some new names or bomb's your chacha: Ishhai Panne, Mohammad Cubed, Goora Walid Shab East, Goora Walid Shab West and the like.

10

Bernadette Aodhfionn

The home is quiet. Usha was what we called her but she was Bernadette Aodhfionn, woman with dark hair and an olive, nearly northern wogland complexion. She and I are talking at the end of a hallway that overlooks the water. She's telling me about her childhood. A group of students were walking home from school on a September afternoon somewhere in County Tyrone, Usha tells me. She says her sister was among this group of friends. Pigtails and skipping home in the autumn air. They were tossing ink projectiles made of tissue paper, splattering on laughing faces.

A car painted flat green that looks like a small tank with large tires pulls over and the soldiers question some of the small children. Usha's sister, who wasn't twelve yet, has been questioned by one of the men in uniform. Had she seen the man in this photo? Had he used this road? How're we supposed to know, Mr. British soldier? Then he offers her his hand to shake, he does not let go and slowly breaks her index finger with a snap. "That's for Ireland. I'm from Hackney," the soldier states. Her sister's open mouth corrupts uglily, her springtime laughter ruptures in a puppy squeal. Tears run down her cheeks. The soldier laughs. The other soldier reprimands:

"We'll get shit for this. You shouldn't have done it. She's only a little kid. Only a kid." They drive off in their green car. Usha's career against the British begins. This memory looms large inside her. Where did it all get her? She's here in the home now—memory not fading, however. Alzheimer's year one, or is it two? She has forgotten what a toothbrush is for. She came to us as an explosives expert and now she asks if we can put 365 days in a toothbrush.

Many years later, after the many things we did together, at home, abroad and here on the silly mainland—she means England—after much reading and training, this twiggy wound of childhood is still a treasure she carries around today, draped in a clear understanding of what has to be done. She's now Usha, but not from South Asia at all. It's just a code name because somehow she had, for an Irish woman, darker than usual skin, and dark hair. The name protects her from the machinery of wrongful imprisonment.

An internship from Terror Central helped her to change her accent to an object of great military value. Yes, accents are of military value. Visitors would come infrequently, but they would come: intelligent men who worked against the castle. She was on the Islamic payroll now, if that's what you can call it and, far be it for her to complain but the international trips had been reduced, and she needed a break from it all to study, and it was going to be very difficult to break suddenly without looking as though she'd crossed over to the other side. Nobody would have believed she would. Would the smart directors of operations look the other way, while she spent more time with her books, did a bit of travelling? Daily, these thoughts echo in her mind. But the breaking of twigs in the middle of night re-commits her to her role as someone who wanted to do something, not just safe and sentimental protests in the streets. Usha, an ordinary, obsequious student of their classics, but an extraordinary student of James Connolly and Ali Shari'ati.

In my room in the home, abruptly, the phone rings. Our conversation stops. I look at the floor; she winks at me, and touches my hand as if to say that the call will be over soon. She has a fatal disease called old age. I absorb the trans-Atlantic call in bits and pieces. I read an article in *The Economist* about scientists still attempting cold fusion. Who's on the phone? It must be her son. She looks at me with her green eyes. "Miracles under the microscope," about how medical science is defeating the science of miracles. Lourdes, the Virgin Mary, the Christian miracles committee of slightly learned men were getting fucked by science.

Her life flows tensely in and out of a small elegant flat in upper middle class London. This particular operation means a long wait after another long wait until the moment when our planning pays off. The programme of activities has gone on for months; she is bored stiff. She occasionally stares at the phone, admiring its uncrackable privacy options. The radio in her kitchen bleats familiar stories that haven't changed since the Persian Wars: it's about maintaining the status quo and securing an internal arrangement. It's about putting in place a unionist dominated Assembly. Till kingdom come.

Her bosses have forbidden any casual English contacts,

and other things that soothe the loneliness of the watcher. Better to die fighting than a wretched gulam. Islam helped these poor Catholics. She has not had one failure in four years of operations. Sometimes, months go by and nothing happens. In these periods she imagines what a certain operation will achieve, what the risks are, could it backfire in the media? What are the long-term goals of these things that we do?

This month, a phone call must arrive. It must indicate that a settlement has been reached. All of the planning is successful if the bits in the phone chip are excited and make the required sounds. Then home forever among the green fields. Perhaps she'll set up a business importing espresso machines to all of Northern Ireland, or become a school teacher and have children.

Was it really she who may have snuffed out the lives of ordinary, decent citizens who abided all their lives by real values? Was it really her forefathers who killed all those horses at a parade? Aside from that Queen Elizabeth, how was the parade? What was her exact role in the bombings? She's a very nice woman, filled with ordinary respectable worries, not one worry too many.

Her nights are filled with long and short underground train rides to bars away from her neighbourhood to prevent English rules of familiarity from applying. Even the daily newspapers have had to be purchased at a safe distance, many tube stops away, and never ever from the same newsagent twice. She has been given a little car, which is infrequently used. Until recently, she had even had time to stay abreast of her studies at a university on the mainland. Had she really dropped out?

Will Europe wait for her to catch up? What was her doctorate on? She'll tell me one day.

The phone is positioned on a small brown wooden table beside the coat rack; it is supposed to be answered only if it rings more than six times. Today on the fourth day of the week, she has been given the clearance to express happiness on her mother's birthday; her little sister, mother of four sons, will have to be called another day.

"Happy birthday, Mum. I miss you. Been thinking about you." Everything all right then love? I'm a terrorist and about to kill many people in London. You'll hear all about it, Mum. I know exactly what I'm doing. I hope one day to bomb the Olympics of Gay and Handicapped People. Five minutes of that. Untraceable. Bye, Mum.

Her black hair flows over pronounced yet delicate shoulders. Her outward morphology is so finely balanced, her politics so undecorated, direct and robust that her Moslem—so called Moslem—bosses avoid arguing with her.

It is now Saturday night, 14 degrees Celsius, two days before her period. Her oval face and a long ski-hill nose with a little bump on its end are waiting for a call that will signal a complete end to this stage of things. However, she requires a savage sexual rendezvous. Clichéd desire, yes, she tells me now at the old folk's home. But she has already started to mentally prepare for an operation within an operation. A jolly good fuck before the splattering of civilians.

She paints her fingernails, her peering half-moons now subdued into reflective red obscurity. A thin tracing of red lipstick; Joan Baez hoop earrings; black jacket.

The grey coat with a sharp, pointed collar, draped over a wooden coat rack with four hooks, will add ten years to her looks; however, the advantage is that when she de-cloaks her tight jeans and black turtle neck will reveal her perennially naive-looking body, which has experienced military occupation.

This sub-operation starts from the corner of Akenside and another nondescript street, then a smart walk to Belsize Lane, right onto Haverstock Hill with its autumnal hedges. Falling temperature. Now: 12 Celsius. Her low black heels stop clicking in front of the houses which have doors of approximately the same colour, beige, one slightly more annoyingly beige than the other. The keys are in her pocket. Double-check. A casual look back at the similar doors. Then along a series of houses with brown hedges still sagging with the afternoon's rain. She draws the grey collar ends tightly around her, then continues walking down into the bright yellow tube stop named Belsize Park. Her intent is to meet someone. She sits at the bar; a Senegalese barman addresses her in local English. She responds in local middle-upper class non-Irish. Moments later, he places a pint of Guinness in front of her. She leaves the change on the counter, finds a round brown table, and peers out of a window that frames trees on a patio.

A youngish, dark-haired man says: "Wonderful view." She looks at him. "The view is nice—do you think this is so because we are close to a university?" she asks. He teaches modern languages. She takes off her coat and slowly places her hands on her blue-jeaned thighs. He finishes his drink.

"Can I offer you another?" What do they discuss? Something so frightfully close to home that it surprises her. There had been a small bombing the previous morning, not a job done by her; he brings it up to demonstrate his knowledge of international politics.

"Well, it is a complicated affair, don't you think?" She shows sympathy for the cause and for that word, *complicated.* Better not be taken for a twit by a fully grown British woolly liberal. She offers him her eyes for the peering. The same ones that I peer into now some three or four decades later. A few not-so-erudite historical examples on the Irish question keep her above him without letting the real goal disappear. "Peace and compromise are the total answer. Our troops must leave. We don't have any business being there at all—what do you feel?"

"Business?" She asks. His hand gently moves his brown hair from his forehead.

The taxi back to her place takes too long. While they kiss, she plays with his balls. She's not allowed to have anyone in the safe house—otherwise, how would it remain a safe house? He freely admits that he has a wife and is not unhappy about it. Rules invite the use of non-rules.

On this moonless night, she need only wait for a few minutes longer before she has his condom inside her. He pays the taxi driver. They walk upstairs to the safe house. The white door of her apartment gently clicks shut. They stand under a yellowish lampshade in the tiny hexagonal hallway. She draws his tongue out under the light and licks it as though it were a detached autonomous republic. She bites and sucks his lips. She brought sex into the safe house. He draws away in surprise. Do I know this man? Is he who I am thinking he is? She is down on her knees undoing his fly. He bends over to touch her waist from behind. She's far too gentle for a mass murderess. Slowly, she stands and turns around; condom-cloaked modern languages are inserted. She can detect his patient wife's training. She has fallen madly in love with him. Perhaps, after the war, this English sod will move to Belfast and have kids with her. She is now eighty and telling me all this. I never suspected this when I knew her during working hours.

Months of pent-up loneliness unfold: her eyelids slowly open and she looks directly back at him. The phone is in front of her; it hasn't rung in days. Her hand gently reaches back to his buttocks to stop him but not to retract. The command is direct and forthright. The phone is ringing.

A melodious voice emerges from Europe: "Hello. Thanking you for picking up on exactly sixth ring. Ha Ha. Efficient. You are well-trained, I must to say. Things have gone well here and there, I hear. How are you?"

"When should I expect you?" she asks.

"Early morning landing in capital of empire, brunch," he replies. She tactfully repeats the word "brunch" for the liberal inside her who acknowledges comprehension by pulling back on her hips.

"Goodbye," she says.

"What happens if I want to see you again?" he asks. She holds him close to her. Promise you'll never leave me. Promise. He walks out into an ordinary morning. She lets the curtain fall back. The sunlight enters her room in the old folk's home. Nothing was compromised.

Two operations in one day. I hear all about the complexity of the Irish question, arms acquisitions, expeditions and love affairs. This is what pulls me to her, at this closing chapter of her life.

"So all is hunky-dory. Usha—nice name I gave to the operation, don't you think? I'll be bringing along a new friend. He can stay with us for a few days?"

"With pleasure," she replies.

I can hear her son shouting on the phone—surely her hearing can't be that bad. I look up at my article on "those involved in the medical process of miracle assessment welcome new scientific tools ..." She freezes in mid-sentence: she's dead. Gone without chatting to the media. God bless her. This is how He takes us: in mid-sentence with a trans-Atlantic son fading in the cochlear implant. Calmly, I take the thin phone from her warm hand and explain to her son James, whom she has told me lots about. As I put the earphone to my ear, I hear him asking: "Mom, are you still there? Mom, are you still there?" Yes, she is still here.

"James, I think your mother has passed out. I'll call a nurse. Hold on a moment. Please. Hold on a moment." I haven't a trace of panic in my voice. I press the buzzer. A nurse rushes in and expertly takes her pulse at the neck and wrist. Er, James. How shall I say this. Yes, James, your mother has left us both. I'm afraid. What are we to do? This is what happens, James. She was pushing the very late seventies or eighties. She was a great mass murderess.

"Are you able to come over to take care of things? I'd like to meet you." I am tempted to add: Your mother and I were friends. She killed many people at my beckoning. She showed me a world, the world. The son is silent for seconds. Exactly what were the chances she would leave on Monday at 10:36 on 14 February? Planets never exactly retrace their orbits. "Yes, I'll come as soon as I can." James watches flakes of snow over the Shannon waves and says goodbye to me. I have her print of Franz Kline—a black and white painting of a bridge without a world underneath it. Just black paint on white paint, that's all it was. I had known this version of his mother for exactly six months, fourteen days and ten hours. Compressing life-times like a spiral arm of a galaxy twisting into a few points. Where will she be in a few hours? They'll be taking out her last breakfast at the embalmers at 15:00.

I think about her at dinner time that same evening. I put a forkful of food into my mouth. I think back on my chat with her son. She's hardly a heartbreak to me. Good while it lasted. I'll look up Tatjana Lucrece down the hall, but before I visit her, I think I'll review material from my past.

Mild Cognitive South

A warm November afternoon hovers outside my window. It's easy to get to my window from downtown Montreal by car or public transportation. The Home Office gave me a pass. From Gare Centrale in Montreal, you take the Deux-Montagnes train going to Roxboro-Pierrefonds where you get off and take the 68 bus. Sometimes, the stations will seem familiar, Gare Centrale, Canora, Mont-Royal, Montpellier, Du Ruisseau, Bois-Franc, Sunnybrooke, Roxboro-Pierrefonds; sometimes they are as new as a baby who doesn't yet have a name. But that religious institution near train stop Mordechai Vanunu has a name and a confessional affiliation. Doesn't it? Oh doesn't it? Sometimes, especially when this happens infrequently, one forgets the stop one is supposed to get off at and suddenly panic fills the brain when I see the following stops glide by: Île-Bigras, Sainte-Dorothée, Grand-Moulin, and finally Deux-Montagnes. At this last stop I have to get off, get another ticket and head backwards in time: Deux-Montagnes, Grand-Moulin, Sainte-Dorothée, Île-Bigras, Mild Cognitive South, Mild Cognitive Roxboro-Pierrefonds and lastly Not-So-Mild-Impairment-North. Sitting directly in front of the map is a good idea, but then I have to coordinate the map with a visual sighting of the station. Alternatively, to challenge the older mind one takes the bus from downtown Montreal to the Fairview Shopping Mall, followed by the 201 bus to my window. Ninety minutes on the 201 to splendour and intestinal vomiting in Pierrefonds. Train stops are like biomarkers that are used to detect our early-onset memory-fade.

Linda—you've given me the keys to your apartment near the park in Montreal and I have taken the 68 to Roxborough to Gare Windsor then the métro to Places des Arts, followed by the 80 bus northbound to Mont Royal. I'm not dreaming this from my home for the aged, am I? Did I really buy a train ticket? Or am I actually in my home for the contemplative with my old friend Anver? I gather that it's apparent that he is Anver.

At any rate all this split-up reality bores me.

I am now thinking about an old girlfriend who was from the dark world where only a certain class has access to democracy—a democracy that transpires in the living room. Linda is not like her. Usha is not like her. From Damascus or Cairo. I tell her you're over seventy-two and you have not moved across town as you said you would. I think I've come to celebrate your birthday, but I'm not sure. You said you'd moved out during the last century. We've decided to age together, haven't we, after all?

The bathroom, in an apartment in the Plateau-Mont-Royal area of Montreal, has small tessellated, hexagonal white tiles. As agreed, the door is left open. I walk in and see the steam issuing from the bathroom. You've left the door ajar, and the sound system on, Bach cantatas and scented steam. Will you have a heart attack if

I come in now and surprise you? I don't want you to die. You'll die if I throw a cold glass of water on you when you're under a hot shower like that. Dear Diary: what's wrong if I admit to having these thoughts?

A fine steam issues from the bathroom. It curls around your childhood photos on the beach, it almost meets me at the front door, which is three metres away from where you are now, basking under hot water. But why isn't a light on? Strange of you. I walk to the door and you smile; you're not going to die at all. I look down and see a list of soap suds going down the drain to eternity. A wan November light falls all over her. She gently rubs soap on herself in a stream of hot shower water. I go to the living room and turn down Bach so I can better see you in the steam. Volume and vision are the same thing in old age: the louder the volume the less clearly I can see things. Then an accident. I touch the wrong dial or button and the radio comes on. Apparently, it's news time: the author of the London Art Gallery bombings, Iqbal Masoume has been ... Thought I'd heard that already. When did I hear it? The last century? The wonders of old age. Why did we bomb all those Francis Bacon paintings? I enjoyed bombing western art institutions the most, but the down side was that there were no injuries at all. The rich got more angry at us for doing modern paintings.

12

Wrinkles

Her breasts in streaming water; thrombotic veins all over her falling breasts. She's standing in the tub, water falling on her long and elegant skeletal structure no longer covered with smooth, olive-coloured skin. Her facial bones prop up the weathered tent of her oval face—the delicate chin. She is beautiful, I always knew that. Light-filled, hazel eyes. One of her hands has dark spots which comically trail towards her armpits. I loved watching her hands pluck fresh coriander leaves. Her lined palms quickly move a few strands of frizzy grey hair out of the eyes; she froths up soap in an ancient and familiar way. Her face gently leans into the stream of water as she washes the suds in distinct white fluid lines down to her armpits. This is the view from the door. You're a little hard of hearing and your hearing-aid is out in the bedroom. You'll place it in your ear after things have dried. When we cuddle we wear our hearing-aids. The amplified sound enters our ears and increases our love for each other. We tried without the chips, but it's no good. Her old age and mine are interlocked in hearing-aid happiness. Are you sure about this, old boy? Really sure that you're really remembering things as they were or are? She lives far away from you now. No she does not, her house is just down the street. I live with her in her home, forty kilometres west on a smooth highway not built by the Romans. Yes, this is right. I live with her. We're growing old together, and are we or are we not living in an old folk's home together?

She has a perfectly healed scar under one drooping breast. I know, I saw it heal day by day, month by month, year by year. An Arabesque fine lattice work of wrinkled skin covers her breasts in cross-hatched lines that radiate outward from her armpits to the top of her hip, where the flesh becomes so dense that it falls over itself. I noted the evolution of this exact droop. The pleasure of aging together. In your fifties your flesh was firm when I touched it; in your sixties it bulged like saturnine rings of orbital fat. The folds actually happened rather recently. Almost suddenly. You see, this is how I've maintained my intimacy with you, I've been watching your body as if I were a camera—John Macleod set to take a fluid series of very fine resolution images every five years. I whiz them through my mind on a daily basis, sometimes faster, sometimes slower, but they are there, these images. Sometimes I make them move, in sequence, fast, sometimes I slow them down so I see the transformation in yearly bits of images without sound. This snap snap of your softening body is my sense of your history: I'm the observer, and when I observe, I control history and its outcome.

I recall, as I too aged, watching you go from firmness to fleshy fluidity. My daily observations of you show me the rate at which you will evolve into small particles. I know you've noticed the changes in me.

She lifts her breasts and soaps them within the folds underneath her nipples. Wrinkles reign over every part of her body. Her crotch—still lovely to me—the valley between her thighs is lined with diagonal, horizontal, vertical wrinkles. One does not view your body as something with a recent past. I don't. The magazines of nude young women have a beauty as well, but age produces a body with a different set of late wrinkle harmonics, a different sexual aggression antagonized by a flesh that yields, or not at all. We've developed together. Her toes, painted, shyly shine through the suds on the floor of the bathtub. Her bowl-shaped hips, now near-translucent folds of flesh, fall everywhere; her buttocks hang down in triplicate, white, creamy terraces seen only on faraway planets.

A man's hand enters the scene—it's my hand and I tenderly touch the small of her back. She looks back at me with fake surprise, and smiles. The hot water catches the fading yellow light falling in from the window. A luminous bead of water rolls down a skin canal; I follow it with the tip of my finger. Dutifully, you wash your crotch. I watch a galactic arm of soapy suds moving down the drain. We hear a man's voice, it's my voice, and I ask: "I like your fins, are you becoming a fish?" Lovingly, the man rubs the soap off her wet body. I see her dentures on the shelf near the sink. Mirrored tenderness: "I'm becoming a fish, yes. And thank you for coming, Joseph. Nice surprise."

Lovingly, I, Joseph Macleod—the same age as her, perhaps older—drape a long white towel around her shoulders. She reaches for the reading glasses she uses despite laser surgery, which now returns your eyesight to when you were eight. Here, let me get those for you.

Underneath your nightgown you're wearing a green pair of shorts or something. When you were younger, I remember the operation on one of your breasts. The doctor said that your breast had hardened due to an infection. I know we don't have any problems like that nowadays. They had to re-cut your breast again and this time they let it heal without stitching it up. You had home visits by a kind nurse who would poke a three-metre-long wick into the gash in your breast to soak up all the defensive pus your body was obligated to produce. The nurse's pus-soaking wick became shorter and shorter as your breast healed. Your breast was like the green on church roofs; the oncologists' slashes in your armpits were a copper-green and flesh-pink. That's what I remember.

"Here are your glasses, my dear."

I kid you about your flesh hanging like fish fins. I'm helping a fellow terrorist age in comfort and affection. We're human beings also.

I touch the small of her back again. Despite the black towel, I gently touch her crotch, your bum, and your nipples following the folds of history. I kiss you. My fingers touch your neck of many folds.

The cold has stripped the trees of leaves, making it a clear morning with a soundless sky. Are we moving toward spring or winter? The Earth's axis has tilted further away from the sun as the cults predicted. Last year, Canberra got thumped with six centimetres of snow, and it didn't thaw out for five days. What, we are moving toward autumn or spring? Are the days getting longer or shorter? I do remember that there was a change sometime in the recent past. But in whose recent past?

13

Prayer bruises

The screen contains no images connected to what the voice is saying. Anver, sometimes, looks at the codex screen as though he were looking for moving images that go along with the voice. Cinematic conditioning, I reckon. To keep Anver amused, I have added still photographs from our initial calculations for bombings. Here he is laughing like a camel in Cairo, and in another he's eating a swine-laden hot dog outside Union Station in Toronto.

Anver is beside me. I press *enter.*

A voice rustles out of the computer:

> *The subway takes us from the cool suburban Maadi to Merigis to the urban Heliopolis, past Sadat near Tarir in downtown Cairo, where many men boast prayer bruises—zebeeb—on their heads, but no more action than a bruised forehead. In a tunnel, the sexy crucifixes of Coptic women catch the train's fluorescent lights, only to be blasted to white as we clear the tunnel into—ascension—sunlight. A young Arab boy sports a knapsack with a button: I heart symbol NY. It's Easter.*

Anver is listening. "Please, John, can we please change the voice accent setting? Somehow this hijacking of the plane doesn't go well with this World War Two voice-over. I am getting tired of those old world World War Two voices that you continually use."

"Alright, how about South West American? Early Black English or contemporary English—sort of from around North Carolina? You didn't need much convincing back then; back then, you and the job merged. You just slid into the job. Bang, bang. You liked it."

"North Carolina? Why that place—no metros there, are there? Why are you now going to use a yank voice-over for your hijacking diary? Americans are idiots who don't want public trains or healthcare for other American citizens; we wanted to spend our last days in the belly of the beast, but we choose Canada, because Canadians are even more stupid. The Americans want individual trains—you know, ones with four seats in them. I mean, really, it's 2040 and the Canadian idiots still haven't installed maglev trains. In chopstickland they have trains that travel at the speed of light."

Anver gives me with a familiar look. "We are more or less fit old men. No one would think that we could correct imperialism so why don't we do something really independent? I mean, why don't we do some damage here or somewhere near here? We're old but we can still do something."

"Why should we? We're old now. No point. Imperialism won—look what it made me do."

"Come off it. We should. Aren't you even going to think about it?"

"What are we going to use? Knives and forks from the kitchen?"

I look at Anver. He continues to look at me. I'm thinking about his proposition as the written diary becomes a North Carolinian voice: Will the Montreal metro change some of its names also? The Prime Minister is thinking of making some changes. The first stop that should be blasted off—sandblasted off that is or double named—is Lionel Groulx. Groulx, that fascist, would have knapsacked all the minorities in Montreal if he were alive. To Knap or be Knapped that is the question. My Kingdom for a Knap, The Merry Wives of Knap, Romeo and Knapp, Knapp's Last Tape. Although there weren't any knapsacks in early human history, Anver would have found something similar. *Homo terrorristicus.*

I look at Anver. "Do you think we could blast that religious place on rue Mordechai Vanunu, in the Plateau area of Montreal? The left-wing people live there."

I say: "Why not something else? Why an innocent religious place? Aren't we too old to even be thinking about this? And how do we get supplies? Why an innocent little ..."

Abstractly, Anver says the word "innocence".

"Should I re-start my literary masterpiece?"

"Dying to hear more."

"More of the diary? You really want to hear more of my diary?"

"Yes, I do want to hear more. And what about Mordechai?"

"Anver, how old are you? We've stopped. Listen, just listen. Get old. Here. Why get excited about something we're too old to do? Forget it. Here, enjoy our youth. Listen."

The voice continues:

> *The Hong Kong metro wouldn't be useful to us, but we explored it nonetheless. Dimitri, Mohammad or Charlemagne gave us tickets and expenses. We didn't have to cloak and dagger to get the money; we just went to their offices on Great Russell Road. There was a sign outside that read: We terrorize rats, mice, ants, and other vermin: telephone 020 7249 5632. We used some of the money to meet prostitutes who ate pork five times a day. Circumcised dicks and pork breath.*
>
> *The trains in HK don't have partitions and are long, hollow, metal snakes that drink water at each station because the geomancer tells them to. These trains would require front-end and back-end knaps with some timing, though I suppose we could wait until the trains were moving along a long straight stretch so the head and tail knaps could see each other when acceleration becomes a derivative of time. Allah-o-Akbar to the snake soup eaters. These Chinese stops do not fit into our mindset; the name-sound-mechanics don't really work.*

Anver interrupts: "Are the stops in sequence? You may want to publish this thing one day."

"Just listen."

Tsim Sha Tsui, Lam Tin, Mei Fou, Fortress Hill and Admiralty. And it would not sound great on the telly—Terrorists Bomb Tsim Sha Tsui or Admiralty. The event would sound much better if it were something like Westminster Bomb Blast, London in Panic.

It's difficult to eat here: wall-to-wall pork. No, it's not difficult at all. So we left them in peace. Besides, they have the dim sum nuke, so no one will touch them.

A train moving in the opposite direction decelerates across my favourite Paris metro stop, Sèvres Babylone—did any one of you get on at this stop today? I ask people in the airplane that we once low-jacked (we forced the non-Islamic pilot to stay at 1000 metres above sea level).

We thought about the Boston T for obvious reasons. It's square, grid-organized, un-European, not a poetic system like Paris. One arm of it gushes out to the airport—where Mohammad Atta took his flight to NYC—with nonchalant-coat-over-the-shoulder Bill Clinton elegance.

"Couldn't have been Clinton."

"You're right."

I don't think any American is going to accept a Boston train stop named Mohammad Atta or Mohammed Ya'nni Kuss-Atta.

"Why so many Mohammads in it?"

"I could change the Mohammads. But to what? Javids? Wouldn't that make it too local?"

"And, I know you're going to mention information you claim to have gotten in the 1980s but that you really got from the web today. This makes your diary inaccurate."

> *Nordic countries were a no go from HQ Wilberforce, U.K. Islam has no midnight sun and they have more human rights types than China. More utterly inconsequential human rights professionals than you can shake a stick at. I have translated the names via an online translation programme.*
>
> *Ruoholahti: Grass Bay; Rautatientori—Railway Square; Kulosaari ... some kind of burning island; Siilitie—Hedgehog Road; Itäkeskus—Eastern Centre; Kontula—this could be the translation for the Hobbits' homestead; Vuosaari—Bay Island in Finnish, North Sea in Swedish, whatever. We were there for twenty-four hours and came back on the tube, Fabians we are.*

Anver again interrupts: "You missed a word, it's the Piccadilly Line."

"Thank you, Anver."

"What were you thinking about, rue Mordechai Vanunu?"

We're always, and I mean always, calculating Far Rockaway, Beach 25 St., followed by the imaginatively titled Beach 36 St. and Beach 44 St. These Anglo-Saxon boiled meat banalities are followed by Grand St. and a Mayflower echo: Brighton Beach.

14

Pilots Integrated with Allah

On a large sea cruiser, we sail through the Arabian Sea at twilight. The call to prayer fades as Karachi becomes a red dot on the horizon. Liverpool. White English kids knee the young Paki's nose in the slum school yard. Broken. Four British citizens with the help of an Egyptian national (recently proven to be innocent) suicide-bomb three underground tube stops and the number 30 bus. The Hollies sang about a bus stop, a girl, and an umbrella. They were referring to the number 30 bus in London. But how could The Hollies have known about the bombing, an event taking place forty years in the future? Rock musicians can be perceptive, eerily clairvoyant, and endlessly humanitarian. A few people were killed. Much ado about nothing, all things being equal—unless, of course, you're an aunt or a father or brother or sister or a mother or a head of state who has to pretend to care.

Career journalists say the Moslems who did the bombing are of Pakistani origin. Their mothers come from the following Pakistani cities: Yaro Lund, Croydon, Bradford, Leeds, Multan, Islamabad. The British authorities are asking Moslem leaders to expose the extremists within their fold. The Islamic leaders will do what is required. Publicly, the Prime Minister told us that the Iraqis had weapons of mass destruction. Some embassies helped us.

Recently, the English crime-solving people tried to blackmail British citizens born in the terrorist countries.

The white world unconditionally supports the Israelis. We are going to fly over a few settlements today. We've asked Tel Aviv control to let us descend to 500 metres. One wrong move and Ben Gurion will come back to life, lips and all. Israelis want land for Holocaust museums and shopping malls where Brooklyners can go shopping. Rock stars raise money for Africa, but Africa is finished, yet still good for Darwinians. Africa is a source for their books, which sell well and give these intellectuals prestige. Some of them love lions, tigers, snakes, and cats more than they love humans. A model of compassion created through an affection for lions, tigers, and snakes. Rock stars, giddy with money, think their twanging guitars will save the world. We should continue stealing their music on the internet and put an end to their Rolls Royces. Does Bruce Springsteen want starving Darfurians to sing "Born in the USA" or "I was born a rambling man"?

Niggers with AIDS, clap your hands with Bruce Springsteen, remember we control the Strait of Hormuz; you need oil to transport that electric guitar from Seattle to Vancouver to Oman.

The British intellectuals—all stupor mundi—who grew up eating chapattis and lamb curry see the suffering of weaker people including North Koreans. This—this whole community affair has nothing to do with Islam really. Democracy has two meanings simultaneously. Simultaneously—this is the key word. Who could have predicted we young Moslems with East and West Yorkshire accents would become the real activists independent of the embassies? Depending on someone else—why do that now? Now? When is now exactly? Democracy means support for policies that promote endless hate and decades of poverty for people without any power for niggers—PFPWPORN-General Command. This is what the democratic process is. Any fool can see that. One can't legally send money to Hamasbergers. But you can send all the money you want to Tel Aviv. Like, this is kosher?

Why did the Hounslow bombers take Turkish Airlines to Pakistan for madrassa studies? Why did they support the Turks? The Turks are Israel's friends. Why didn't they fly PIA: "Perhaps I Arrive" or "Please Inform Allah" or "Pilots Integrated with Allah"?

You don't have to be as smart as Edward Said or a whiz kid like Noam Chomsky to see through this? Doktor Said could play the piano and tennis and he banged a major literary critic from Ulan Bator. Really, you don't have to play the piano or be an Egyptian-Palestinian tennis champ to see any of this. He played tennis with a famous tennis player and lost. MI5 won't win either. The bang in London happened. This means they lost. MI5 are stupid pigs with posh-to-not-so-posh accents and degrees in linguistics from Oxbridge. Last fucking Oxbridge cunt I met could not spell jeeehad in Arabic. In the earlier post World War Two recruitment years they could write Arabic. But the PM takes the cake for stupidity. We have no intention of offing him. His final humiliation will be to legislate underground name changes for better cultural integration. PM, we are going to teach you a lesson that the Prince of Wales might understand before you will. Change the tube names or else we'll bang your wife. And it's that kind of bang not the other kind of bang—a bang that will get more minorities jobs doing weather reports on the television or something like that.

Many blacks—even ones who have been denied education—now realize that they were pulled by their vaginal lips onto wooden ships. There will be black suicide bombings if the whites in power don't become politically correct as per our standards.

Usha's in her apartment in London. She looks at the cell phone. A prolonged stare at the phone produces results: four earth shattering rings. "Hello," the friendly telephone voice says.

"They said do it? Yeah, you too, thank you. All okay? The location has been changed to neela tuttay. He is supposed to be ... at another underground stop. Which one?"

"Yeah. So I'll call you later to give you address in London ..."

"You know exactly where that is? You'll tell me more when I get there." It's an old person who answers the phone—a bit of a story left behind in my mind. Happens all the time, sometimes even with childhood friends. The twenty-first century memory pills take all the bugs out of the diskette of the previous century.

"Good morning. How are you? Joseph?"

"Who is speaking with me?"

"Your doctor. Keep things together for a moment, we've some tests to do."

"I was pleasantly distracted for a few moments. Personal history. What's in the newspaper today? I'm fine, thank you for asking."

"We have to do another test. Nothing serious."

"What's serious at this stage?"

"Just in case you live to two hundred years of age," Linda says pleasantly.

"Do you see me as just another patient?

"No. But you're my patient."

Joseph Macleod asks: "How can I be both? I'm your friend first right?"

Linda looks at a book in the room. "What's that book you're reading?"

"Nothing. It's there just to attract your attention. They say old folks here sometimes fall in love."

"You don't need to attract me with books. I like you without the books."

"Propaganda for the home. Loving nurse-client relationship."

"Can I take you for a walk outside?"

"Let's go. Where shall we go?"

"What'll you lecture me on today—local or global politics?"

My nurse could go to the pearly gates before she gets to my age, perhaps in a car accident. I am still, even at my age, filled with pursuits. The other geezers were bankers or wives of geezer-bankers who still paint their nails. Bankrupting tissues—effects of the genotype on aging. See I'm reading about it all the time, as I wither.

I'll check my e-mail now, because I've not done so for days. Here is one I didn't send:

My Dearest:

Why am I writing you again? In a distant way I felt the pain you must have felt. I'll write again. Your occasional e-mails are manna from terrorist heaven. How's your life by the water? Lots of sunshine?

Your Joseph

I fold the codex and let the Muzak version of the Rolling Stone's "The Last Time" bleed into my ears. A sunny summer day at a home's small bowling green. An elderly person's foot taps. Geriatric shoes. Geriatric skin. Balls rolling on the green lawn, crippled hands picking up balls. Breakfast, lunch, dinner, purgatory, hell or heaven.

A tall, black nurse who has gone from man to woman, whom I don't know, walks over to where I'm sunning myself. Now she's gone and Nurse Linda enters the room.

"Brittle winter day, obviously. Is this my five o'clock? Metallic multicoloured pills. Which tract is clogged now?"

Nurse Linda is sombre today. "It is not for a clogged tract."

"Okay fine."

After a tactical pause—a few seconds. "Another detective called for you. He's trying to get information from me. I'll guard your secrets well. I know them all."

"Silly, what secrets do I have? They have nothing better to do than worry about something that happened years ago?"

"If we are to have a friendship, then you must let me play a role in your life," she says.

"Okay, play the role of a woman who is sexually with a father figure, electrolysis of nurse."

"You're a nasty man."

"Who's paying me to love you?"

"No one's paying to love you," she says. Affectionately, she leaves my room. I hear the sea outside. Maybe it's just the ear chip charging. The chip works with light. Ears get lots of light. The uneventful waves gently slap at the hull; the shoo-shoo of the night wind enabling the refuge of sleep. Sleep, of course, but not without my headphones.

Talk to me in a working-class London drawl.

> *The time for multi-religious suicide bombers is on the horizon. We are just at the beginning. Nicaraguan liberation Catholics, Bolivian class-strugglers, Sikh goondas, and Colombian coke growers who don't like Americans flying down from think tanks in Washington D.C. and privatizing their rain water will eventually see the power of the radius. Why should we use Gandhian tactics when you don't?*
>
> *Whites have produced such smart people as Erwin Schrödinger, who showed us a dead cat and an alive cat at the same time. This trick is easier to do with two Korans. He said that the superposition of a dead cat and living cat in a quantum state means that a cat is alive and dead at the same time. No Arab has done this. Certainly not with camels in a superpositioned dual Hellenized quantum state. Riyadh superpositioned over Washington, Washington superpositioned over Riyadh. Dead camel in between. Border controls and ID cards will, in fact, make things easier. We already have so many ID cards that we could construct an airplane with them.*
>
> *This isn't the old days of dealing with an IRA Paddy-puppy army whose members had their last Guinness at room temperature. With*

the belt, or the knapsack, or a duffle bag things aren't at room temperature. Islamic intellectuals translated the Greeks for Europe. Europe wouldn't have TGVs or particle accelerators if the Arabs hadn't translated Socrates for them. From Iberia, the Islamic scholars carried these old translations to the British Library in duffle bags.

A political scientist at a Chicago university thinks that these are not religious acts but political ones.

Obama thinks these are religious acts. Both, Obama and this Chicago professor live in the same America at the same time, just like a dead and living cat.

We sound that religious to you?

15

Van Gogh

I hear another sound that drives me around the bend: the sound of Christmas carols, and of course, the tinkling of spoons against ornate china cups that guilt-ridden sons and daughters offer their parents. Oh, so slowly do they stir. My breathing is slow. Our collective breathing is slow. Our collective urine is fast. The asthmatics are kept elsewhere. No they are not; we all live together.

The singalongers should be set aside, or should have a bowling ball lobbed at their heads. Bastards. The asthmatics have access to oxytaps at every corner—all bronchial congestion is gone for up to forty-eight hours. The geezers say that you could go to one of the three eternal places in the next forty-eight hours with previously congested lungs now working as clean as whistles, arriving at the pearly gates with clean lungs, and blackened souls.

I blame, again, the guilty children. I've no children, so I must be jealous. Really, I have no children? Ah come on. What about that woman in the airport? The smell of old age urine, medicines, and cleaning chemicals annoys me. Squeaky wheelchairs add to my hearing loss. Even with the modern hearing-aid. Their squeaking erodes my eardrums. But I keep hearing them more and more clearly. Can my hearing be improving? Is there a new pill for deafness? Nowadays, yes, there's a pill—an ear pill.

Our hallways are broad. Large majestic reproductions of Cézanne or Van Gogh in his Arles-or-something-like-it phase don't impress me. We have a pretentious director of this home for the aged, the dying, and the voluntarily non-contemplative. No shortage of this last group.

One old man buzzes by them on his motorized wheelchair. The wheelchair buzzard leaves a trail of art historian urine. He's drooling from the mouth, tearing along, loudly pronouncing all the names of all the painters in the long hall: "Cezanne, Renoir—*Dejeuner sur l'herbe, The Raft of the Medusa*—with blacky on top, Pissarro—too many dots ... too many dots ..." Our home director had a thing for the 19th century European painters.

I never thought I'd continually see trees swaying in the south of France to the smell of old age, and a view of the Saint Lawrence River marking off the days. This art historian life ends. I want to go to Montreal for a medium smoked meat.

I have not quite closed my codex: a voice emerges asking me if I am sure I want to shut down. It is a voice with an accent I've never heard before. It's a computer manufactured voice, the pull down menu on the screen offers:

Select geographical accent:

The pull-down menu offers two hundred choices of current countries in addition to another hundred voices for countries in different historical eras.

Select accent voice layering accent:

Three hundred choices, by country. I've selected a downtown, working-class Port Moresby accent, layered with California Valley Girl, I kid you not: this is actually a choice my codex offers. And for background sound, I've selected nineteenth-century train whistles.

> *Please allow me to return to that plane we hijacked. This is exactly the kind of old-fashioned terrorism we don't want to conduct any longer. It is messy and anti-intellectual, and turns the West against us; ideally we want to do things that will make the West like us more.*
>
> *We want to—or rather it is not a question of want so much as need to—invent new ways. We took photos of ourselves with the passengers, some of whom resented this. People in these kinds of situations want to retaliate against us—I can see it in their eyes. A Finnish woman of forty-five, with blond hair and an hourglass body, seated in row 21 seat C—travelling alone to a vacation resort in the darker parts of the world referred to our photos as trophy photos and found us rude. The word "rude" hurt me. I mean, does she not find all the inequality in the world rude? I mentioned this to her while I was patrolling the A380. As I confidently walk the aisles she adds: "Surely, there must be other ways to address your problems?"*

"Aren't my problems your problems?"

"Your problems are your problems"

"Perhaps I will have a problem if the army arrests us all when we land."

"Where are we landing, then?"

"Where are we landing? Where they can't arrest us. If they arrest us, we will kill many people in their cities."

What we are doing is called terrorism, but as you can see this is not terrorism; it is a kind of near-tourism. Passengers, you are now part of "Operation Balance Israel." The current head of the U.K. has banned showings of The Battle of Algiers—a film we saw in Kandahar, during our graduate studies, I mean our real graduate studies, so graduate that some of us didn't come back for further earthly studies. The current head of the U.K. is spending ten million extra to protect his elected members of parliament. We're having an effect. We have degrees in literature, history, chemistry, and queer studies and we even know a bit about a Russian poet who always wore yellow shirts.

Do your soldiers have funny accents? No. Neither do we. We're the New Islamo-Model Army. Right on your doorstep. Right here beside your red top milk bottle. Ah, here is the chief of your airport now addressing you. A tense silence like the one that Mullah X786 used to instil in our classes now exists in our captured plane.

His image appears on all the seat screens. A grey man in his early forties calmly states: "We are unable to prevent take off. We regret this. They—they have asked me to use the word they, and this exact text has been written by them. They have surrounded many airports, Hong Kong, Heathrow, O'Hare, Ben Gurion and Charles De Gaulle with nuclear bombs. We've given them clearance. We regret this. They said they regret this also. I have been asked to read it all to you."

I use the address system:

"Hello passengers, Sandra Qureshi directly from the tribe of Mohammad (PBUH) will offer you some pork-free food as soon as we're in the air. It'll be the very first flight you will take without those boring emergency demonstrations. Madame Mazlooum to my left with the Uzi is not veiled and is wearing a modest mini. Would you like me to continue with my A-rab accent or ought I to continue with my normal Lake Districtesque English? I see a few nods. Okay, Lake District it is. Please to tell me yanne. Qwais. We've arranged for you to watch Lawrence of Arabia, One Night Stand, and/or Harry Potter with wog subtitles. In the hold we are carrying the Elgin Marbles with parachutes. You have our permission to use your cell phone to make calls for the duration of the flight."

Anver interrupts: "You've mentioned cell phones. This is false."

"Anver, this is a personal diary of our past—surely I can make up a few things."

> *And now, it is time for takeoff. And for anyone whose battery power has run out we can offer you one of our phones. By special arrangement we will fly low sometimes as low as 850 metres. You'll get a better view of the cities—cities, which, as one of your progressive gay and lesbian French historians writes are always stages in the preparation for war. This view of cities and the land will give you a unique once-in-a-lifetime flying experience—thanks to what you might call terrorism. Use your cell phones and tell your friends and loved ones that you are fine. Here are the phone numbers to the main newspapers—send them photos: we'll pose with your children if you want. I want to be on the front page of* The Telegraph *hugging one of the kids.*
>
> *Notice the Harriers starboard side? Watch, I'll make them drop their course. Imram Khanmann, dear. The vector-thrusted Harriers fall from view. What's worse: being hijacked or listening to my stories?*

16

Teleportation

It's Monday afternoon: singalong time. My wrinkled mouth makes the required sounds. Why should my wrinkled mouth make the sounds? Hell with that. I walk away. However, within myself, I protest, and I shall in writing. I have a petition in hand. No, I don't. It is all in my head. No physical petition. Yes, I'm very capable of making the sounds for the singalong. A Beatles song. People in this century are fond of dismissing things that happened a few years ago by saying that something or another happened in the last century. Well then, what is the name of the song? Now, what would be suitable to sing at an old folks home? Rigby something? Martha Rigby, no, that's not it. Must be Michelle Rugby. Guess again, old man. No, it is *Yellow Submarine.* And we've—no they've—been singing this song all week. I am thinking about complaining to the director. I'll get a petition together after all. I want to be entertained. I know I'm way over seventy, but what can I do if I don't march with this petition. Grin, geezer. And I will not sing Yellow under the waves of Britannia. Yellow World War Two, sausages with windows under the ocean blue. What old geezers are going to sign my petition? Geezers, that is forbidden. The Forbidden City of Geezers. Words offend, but I never get offended, because I've an education.

Birds twitter on the fertilizer-driven lawn in a summer afternoon. I can see a few bowling balls clanking against each other. This is my last rendezvous with the literary world of the personal diary. My thought filled life diminishes.

The nurse comes into the false-sun-filled room to give me my three o'clock; she's young, the sun never sets for her. Endless blossom, born in the last century, or so she says. She should be promoted to head nurse, because she gets emotionally close to the residents. Biologically speaking, we are at the beginning of the human clone era and, in the news, there is vague scientific talk of teleportation.

Someone in Hong Kong moved a wonton to Macao via a telephone line, or via satellite or something. I'm sure that's what I heard on the news. The oil companies are very interested in this way of moving goods. Why? Well, because there are insurance fees: the scientists tell us it's so flawless that nothing ever gets damaged. Someone in California is trying to move a mouse to New York with stringweb, mouse to satellite and back. I'll see it when I believe it. Our goal was to demolish this empty capitalism which took a mouse from one hemisphere to another; we wanted badly to replace capitalism with something nicer; sure we were prepared to use some capitalist modes of production but we had had enough of this global neoliberal mouse-eat-mouse-ism. We were and are to this day for the collective ownership of production. Before boarding any flights for distant operations, I lectured my unit about capitalism before, during, and after every operation.

17

Servant

Usha walks into my room in the middle of day. Will she die today while talking on the phone to her son or has that already happened? I think she is sitting in front of me showing me her family photographs. I have taken to Earl Grey and its aroma brings her back, not as the Irish woman with her son James across the pond, but as another woman whom I knew.

Here's what happened a few minutes before her departure: We are sitting chatting in her room looking at photos of her past, some as crinkled as mountain ranges on an old globe. She takes the photographs with shiny black and white surfaces out of the box. Because of the sunlight falling into her room, I have to tilt them to get a clear view; otherwise the content of the photos is obliterated. Moving the photos out of the sunlight adds drama to seeing them.

"When was this taken?"

"This one with me in the navy blue V-neck sweater? Yes, that's me. What did you want to know? This is me when I was engaged in Cairo. That's my boyfriend beside me. He now works at the Asian Bank in Manila. Lots of smog there now, I wouldn't want to live there."

Her shaking hands present me with another photo:

again sunlight clears away the content until I tilt it away from the sun.

"This one's by the seaside?"

Delicately, she turns the less-than-palm-sized photo over and reads: Photo studio, Alexandria, nineteen something, something, something.

"Scared to tell me your age?" I ask, touching her knee. She passes me another nearly faded one in colour.

"A servant?"

"She was like family. We took her on vacation with us. Not so sure if she had an idea what a vacation was. She is dead."

"Yes, vacations. Do you think we're having one now?"

"This servant—all dressed in a *galabaya*—we loved her: we went through many servants. One from the Sudan. She died." Usha sips her tea. The scent wafts by my nose. I offer her a cookie.

"Diabetic. Don't you remember?"

"What's this? A class trip to upper Egypt?"

"Yes. Lovely, isn't it? There's Nina Berunie, Huda Lufti, Saleem Kiddy, Rasheed Nadeem, la petite Italienne, Carla Florenteno, Patrick the English diplomat's son. He had a Scottish accent. I slept with him due to Nassar's revolution. He was circumcised. Raoulf, in the corner, that one is married and now has three children in their sixties. Our families were friends. His sons and daughters visited me, you know. But that was when you weren't here. Yet. Or was that when you had gone to England and were coming back by ship. I don't remember, do you? I remember you called from the ship or from somewhere. Here's another. In colour."

"Were you at university, or high school when this one was taken?"

"This was second-year university. Here's another one of a religious aunt. Have I already shown you the one of the religious aunt? Lovely bonnet or cowl. Do you want more tea? She never got married. I remember remembering her. And there's my father. Banker. Kind banker. You'd have liked him."

18

Frankfurt School

Everyone is sleeping. A few night nurses are on duty. They don't wear white uniforms at night; that's how forward-looking this home is. I'm in my room. My clock freezes for sixty seconds at twenty-three hours and thirty-two minutes. I'm not sure if I've been talking to Anver or Iqbal—who is Iqbal anyway? Was it today or the night before? I walk down past rooms 259, 260, 261 to his room, or let me ask myself if I was walking back to my room after having already visited him earlier today, because things don't seem to be in order: rooms 261, 260 and 259? Sequentialism and its discontents.

Iqbal falls asleep later than the others, like me. The home is filling with night sounds: a blood-filled cough way down the other end, a Frankfurt School snoring from 259, buckets of blood coming out from 261. Nurses are slipping and sliding all over it. The scene fades to old-age black. The wall-to-wall carpet on the second floor where they do routine tests is grey with tiny threads of pink and blue like an intestine opened up at a metro stop. Guts meshed in marble. All the other floors are some kind of stone faux-marble or granite or something cheaper. It's easier to clean a hard surface than a carpeted one. A few weeks ago, I think someone spilt some blue liquid on this faux-marble floor.

I'm in my room sitting beside the window. The snow-covered carpet outside looks like something fluffy at Walmart. I get up and walk down the hall, which is being repainted a faint blue; it's night time—the people painting the halls have left. A section of the shiny concrete floor, or whatever kind of stone, is covered with a green plastic tarpaulin; this makes my slippers sound different than walking on the shiny floor. My hearing-aid catches rustling plastic the painters use to cover the floor. This is the second time I hear the sound of my footsteps change today. Quite an event. I am—with due respect for chronology—coming back from Iqbal's room. Yet, now, suddenly, Iqbal is lying on his bed looking directly forward. Thought you'd died?

"Hello, John," he says.

I am moving out of my own dream into Iqbal's world. But is Iqbal's world in my dream? How could I be moving out of my dream into Iqbal's world without both of us being in my dream?

"Just thought I'd come to say hello. It's late and quiet and ... hear that loud snoring coming from that open door?"

As I talk to Iqbal, my mind wanders off from Pierrefonds to the Plateau-Mont-Royal. This wandering off business is not to be controlled—I ride with it. The pills cause it. I don't let it upset me. Part of my mind engages in memory lane chit-chat with Iqbal, another part of my mind lives my past life. As one proceeds into old age, one gets to enjoy this several-windowed view of past and present. Of course, it does not happen all the time, and it isn't always nice. It is ugly to handle a split-up mind, even if it lasts only a few minutes between doses.

"You're right, that snoring sounds like planes leaving the tarmac."

It starts off as a feeling of elation, then there are two pictures, two worlds separated by an instant. Alzheimer's world is being defeated, small second by small second. We want to remember. Until when do we want to remember? Do we choose what we want to remember or does it all just come inside? Actually, it's more than two pictures at the same time.

I'm in a high-rise apartment in Montreal; the large window gives a wide view of the mountain in the middle of the city with a gigantic, ugly, electric crucifix on top. Moslem background or no, putting up a crucifix on the last remnants of a volcano seems as crude as putting up a mosque in the centre of Berne, or putting Berne in the centre of Bamiko. Like having two or more languages in my mind, words stuck on red foxes that run in clockwise and not-so-clockwise circles. Then the wordfoxes stop, the pills are doing it, thank you science for relaxing the foxes. In a controlled fashion, I redirect my mind back toward the presence of Iqbal, who is now adjusting the small light beside his bed, which is identical to mine. In fact, we all have identical bedside lights. Maybe we're all identical terrorists. One terrorist is just like another one.

"Joseph, give me some water please." I pour, from a glass jug with small bubbles in the water, a long draught like an air steward. I hand it to him. "Do you think that all those years of drinking water with ice in it harmed our collective livers?" What language did he ask me the question in? He has foxes as well.

"Collective livers? Do you mean that we've been sharing one liver in our new home?" He's in form tonight.

"Tell me something, if Joseph, you did get me into the bombing stuff, how'd you convince me? And if you did, why and how did we end up in the same old folk's home? Are you here to make sure that there won't be any deathbed confessions? Why are we so familiar with conventional military words? Must it mean that the state sanctioned our efforts, or that the state needed highly cultured types to do their dirty work? Citizens who think their state won't one day harm them should be gassed. Just a few inaccurate thoughts to keep the truth in order."

Iqbal has a much slighter frame than Anver and has the brown skin as per job requirement, and short white hair. He gets out of bed and walks to the moonlit window. I put my arms around his shoulders. The moonlight flows over his face as it did during one operation when rain was flowing down his face. He was wearing a suit with flip-flops. Flip-flops during an operation? Yes, it's true. As we peer across to the small bay in the river, Iqbal looks at me. "Look at the trees, they look so silvery."

19

Ha'sha'shin

Day after day, as my skin ages, snow falls behind the newspapers that I am reading. Of course, there are no newspapers as such these days—what I'm reading are old newspapers that are placed here for decoration.

Familiarity sets in with the old folks. Usha talks with me about an insurance policy—an insignificant matter, she assures me. She leaves to make phone calls. Night falls on the river, and things are black and blue and Canadian outside. The white days, like a retina, detached from Islamic time. Usha is sitting beside me while I watch the snow behind the newspaper. We hear loud snoring coming from down the hall. Usha looks at me and smiles.

Sunlight deflected off the moon falls through the Venetian blinds, forming a ghostly blue interference pattern on the wall. Usha asks me about my maybe-Oriental eyes. I give genealogical explanations starting from the Palaeolithic era, which the *Ha'sha'shin* dominated.

I'm walking along a hall—I think it's the east-west hall. "Does anyone want any lemon flavoured mineral water?" Who just asked me that question? A busy nurse passes me as I walk along the hall. "Nurse, did you just ask me about mineral water?"

In the morning, Iqbal and I have coffee and get more friendly, like we used to be. He's so old he's forgotten what he did. Iqbal is nearer the pearly gates than Anver. I have to stay here in case he or Usha blows our cover on a full moon night—full moons have an imaginative pull on the truth. Sometimes, due to failing memory, we have to become re-re-acquainted. I open with a question that would be considered normal under the circumstances.

"What did I do to get here?" Iqbal asks.

"Here? Where is here?" I ask him.

Gently, I guide him away from the moonlight. "Would you like some hot weak coffee with milk?" Iqbal is wearing, as he sometimes chooses to, a black silk *shalwar kameeze* with a border octave of violet and blue. After a few minutes: "I would love some coffee, but we have to go to the small kitchen to get some, don't we? I mean—I mean, now that lunch and breakfast are over. Let's go, shall we?" We walk on the green drop cloth, smelling the fresh paint. I place a cup of hot weak coffee in front of him. He says he wants to piss. I hold a cup in front of my fly. He laughs.

"That's a good idea."

He hands me his cup, which I set down on the table. "We did some good things, didn't we? They needed a response, didn't they? Isn't that right, Joseph?"

"If that's true, then that's years ago, and besides, Iqbal, we're friends now, don't you think? Look would anybody but a good friend come to chat with you at 10:58 on a Tuesday morning, and make you coffee—weak under the circumstances—and offer you his only pissing pot? Now, tell me how I got you to end up here?"

Iqbal stalls for a moment till the right story courses through his mind. They have been kind enough to take me for a walk. We left the mosque in London, or was it Mississauga at three in the morning. No one in the elevators, down to the underground parking lot and off to a small country house. "This was a great risk we took ... a great risk bringing you out here," one of the Mohammads told me. He didn't travel with us on the ship.

I'm once again sitting in my room reading my e-mail from August, early in the new century:

My Dear:

Leaves turn to bright red, orange, fall off carpeting over the grass; another day it snows. Along Avenue du Parc, park side. Stripped trees ...

Your call on my cell amid a virginal snowfall. Simple conversation. Routine. Lovers of a different kind, lovers nonetheless. We still share the same streets. I walked past your house near that park. No lights. Must have been sleeping.

I live alone now. I'm used to living alone, or almost that. With an endless stream of mates in a safe house: year after year. A new face, new accent, this time what was it? An Australian from Queensland who received, with ugly regularity, envelopes with stars in a circle. Frosty autumn. Now, years move in blocks of decades. An Arab student. Project partners are a conception of time. Two Scottish linguists in a row. A geographer, a perfect idiot historian, more students, though, never an architect. Then, we interviewed an artist who moved in. Sallow complexion. Moronic ideas. About everything. But she knew how to make das bombs.

Then some money came from somewhere, and I started to live alone in the same house, not far from yours. It all went very well, but I felt that something was missing.

You'd only call once in a while. No eye contact. End of operations. That airport was just a stage between us. I understood. Didn't want complications either. Then, very slowly, something strange happened. A flood of years living alone followed. Are they still good at cricket? You moved out of the country for a while, then back here. I saw your apartment window on a cloud-covered night. Your shadow on a curtain, a blind not fully drawn. Perhaps I'll quickly glimpse a long-fingered hand moving a cigarette to your mouth on 18th of July at 21:32. And, did you or did you not on the first of May at 22:49 cross the living room floor toward the window to water the plants?

Then, it hit me: I was able to pinpoint what that emptiness in my life had been. I now could say what troubled me all these years of not having you in my life. It was not the lack of your physical presence that was difficult to deal with. I knew you were there. After all, we still share the same city, don't we? This was enough to soothe me, because I could always walk past your house. That's how I began to see things from outside your house. What was bothering me all those years? Guilt for having left you? Sorry, I left a few days after the airport life. Guilt for having vanished. No, that feeling is, in one's later years, easy to control and repress to oblivion. Guess what it was? It was simply this: I had begun to miss the presence of a stranger in my apartment —the younger ones, learning to learn things from me.

I'll write again when I hear your voice on my cell.

You are my beloved because you can see the enormous pity I evoke. I left the airport only to be in them all the time. Sometimes I want to move to Mars. Not sure there is much Islam on Mars.

I am in a panic today. I close the computer and put it away. I walk hurriedly. I've seen the doctor; he says I've palpitation of the sagging testicles. I eat hurriedly. I can't stop thinking about her, what life and happiness I could have had with her. Who am I thinking of? Why didn't I stay with her? We could have aged together, learned each other's habits; we could have been supportive of each other. I just don't understand myself these days. Why do

I shake? My health is fine, then why do I shake? All the doctors here know that I am in fine health, but I am alone, and what's the cure for that? Pills? But pills always exist in a collectivity—they are always together in a clear plastic jar. I look at the blue pills near my bedside table. The blue pills resemble the white falling star streaks we see these days. I see about fifty every single night—not falling stars but old satellites falling out of orbit and heading earthward. Or perhaps it's OT—orbital terrorism?

20

Toothbrush

A wind causes the leaves to flap against each other, making sea sounds. Outside my window, two old people have discovered nature: after a lifetime of having discovered nothing at all—we were once bankers or terrorists—they are noisily discovering mushrooms directly beneath my window. Now, what would happen if I drop this potted African violet on their heads? What would it feel like on the noggin? That could be murder. Am I obligated to commit both statutory rape and murder in my golden years? What would a falling toothbrush do to their skulls? Yes, that would be considered an accident. Maybe I'll send my chattering dentures down on their heads? But I was just cleaning my spring-loaded false teeth and they fell on Mrs. Garibaldie's neck and now she has marks.

In the dining room, I can look at nothing else: I focus on forks and knives slowly cutting food on plates and slowly rising to mouths. Sunlight sparkles off expensive jewellery and sinks into the folds of skin. The aged eat light. Maybe I should start a jewellery collection. A jewellery collection without the skin? I could start selling it all to help the aged poor who will never see the insides of homes—palaces—like this one.

Computer-driven wheelchairs with silent electric motors move a mouth close to or farther away from a plate. I eat a grilled cheese sandwich with mango chutney; the latter is my own property. I have brought it from my room, and I am willing to share it with all you fucking idiots. But all these idiots are obsessed with anal fissures, which are really broken sphincters, haemorrhoids to infinity. A geezer said that he hated his broken arsehole so much that he wanted to fling everyone into OT.

After a late lunch, I walk fast back to my room. Linda is there waiting for me.

"What's your fascination with that toothbrush?"

"What makes you think I am fascinated with it—ah, yes, I am forgetting to tell you aspects of my life. Yesterday, when we were in her room, Tatjana held up a toothbrush and asked: 'What's this for? It looks so familiar, but I can't remember what I used it for. Tell me. And please, please don't tell any one I asked you. You saw me looking at it this morning?'"

"It's just that I noticed you looking at it for a long time." She pauses. "Oh, so you've been visiting Tatjana again?"

"Yes, I can't get what I want from you so ..."

"Jealous I am."

Then my loyal nurse pauses before she asks the next question: "Was there much money involved?"

I give her my let's-talk-about-it-later look, but continue on a subject that interests her. "Shall we go for a walk? Yes, there was tons of money involved. This regime wanted it to look as though a wealthy chap like me organized the whole thing. They did not want to be blamed. And I held up my end of the deal—the Arabs—morons the lot—did not get any of the blame. There's not much in the way of motivation, if that's what you're after. Yes, a bit of ideology, but it was money more than anything else. Now, where to for that walk?"

We have left the confines of the home, and we're now on a gravel path that takes us to a small main road. We climb a small hill. We look back at the home; the west wing, like a flat concrete tongue, dips into the river, while the east wing overlooks a green square lawn. Small trees have been planted by the river's edge in case baby Moses appears.

"Did you chat much with her? Tatjana. Doesn't our home look like the Pentagon from up here?"

"I don't think she's very talkative, at least not with me. The Pentagon has more sides."

"How much time do you give her? It's not a question of sides. I get a Pentagon feeling when I look at it from up here," I say.

"Another century, maybe more," she says, smiling.

"Honestly, you think she'll live that long? Maybe she'll live forever."

I'm in the mood to impress Linda. I regurgitate something I recently read in netnews:

"Japan is already one of the world's greyest societies, with 16.7 per cent of its population older than sixty-five. Only Sweden, with 17.6 per cent, is greyer, and Japan is expected to take first place soon. One in four Japanese will be sixty-five or older, and by 2050 that will rise to one in three ... See how well those memory pills are working? I can remember all that. Remember six months ago I was having problems? Triumphant state of mind I have had in these last few years."

"What last few years—want me out of a job? Those are frightening figures. How will I find anyone to marry if all the eligible bachelors are your age?"

"Marry me."

"I may have to accept your offer one day."

We have reached the peak of the little hill outside the old folks home, which has two floors, the top floor has pink walls, the first floor where I live—not far from Tatjana, not far from where Usha lived—has white walls with large windows in front of reception. There is a fat nurse at reception.

It is the 5th of July. We walk back to the home not saying much. A chirpy sentence here and there, nothing much. We walk past the reception. No, we did not walk past reception. Linda and I re-entered via the side door, I think. I remember kitchen noises and the smell of onions being fried. Jean was there. I said hello to him: so did she. So, we came in through the side door. Usha is coming back to me. Something is hurting me; it's not my memory of her. I just talked to her. No, I was in love with her. No one saw us come in. Linda comes to my room: we're having Earl Grey. Linda sees me vanish into myself. There's nothing she can do. She touches my hand: suddenly I think of the owl outside Tatjana's window. "I really wish she'll live forever. Linda, did you notice fatso at reception when we came in?"

"We came in through the side door?"

Ah, the pleasure and sadness of Earl Grey. She stays on a bit longer. "Nice grey flannel pants I have on. Are they new?"

Powerless to initiate any further conversation, I ask pathetically: "More tea?"

21

Gasoline, guilt

My body is fine, so why do they treat me as though I were going to the pearly gates at four o'clock this afternoon? I don't have any panic attacks. Why do I suffer from guilt? Guilt for having pulled Usha or Tatjana into doing things with us? Can I feel guilt for them? I made their lives meaningful. Otherwise, who else would have listened to them for hours? I gave meaning to these women by listening. These women know a listener: I'm a listener alright. Right, a listener until Linda gives me more pills. Linda leaves for a few minutes. I crumple up a piece of paper tight, as tightly as I can, and put it down on the desk beside me; then I turn up my hearing aid—the one I can wear in the shower without getting electrocuted—and I listen to every little stage of the paper trying to become an uncrumpled sheet again. When it first uncrumples, it sounds like what? Sounds like the sea, that's what. Which sea? The lake outside?

Here in Pierrefonds, it's a bone-cracking Montreal winter day. In fact, so cold that it's thrilling. Because it hits the lungs at once, I decide to go out for a walk. Something has changed: a month has just become another month or has a year suddenly become two, or maybe even three? I'm certain of one thing: that it is five o'clock, because the nurse comes to give me my five o'clock. At the end of my life, a major event of the day is seeing metallic multicoloured pills that eventually sail down my throat to the lower Atlantic within. This will keep my tract open.

"Oh, which tract?" I ask Linda.

"Just take it," she says, joking. She is my only real friend here. All the others I mention are people I worked with. And I confess that I don't want them to confess about it all due to depleting marbles. But need I say that again?

"I'm not about to croak. Not this afternoon anyway."

What were my intellectual pursuits? Oh, they were fun. In a way of looking at things: Head of an academic department, I was. I tell her all this, because she asks. No it was not fun. Then she laughs. Stupid academic in-fighting. 365 days of the year: the liberals vs. The Liberals vs. the people who really know things. Foxes and hedgehogs. This makes her really laugh. I ran the most important Islamic studies department in the world. Yes, that's true, it's true. She smells ever so lightly, touched with a field of not very redolent flowers, fox or mink bladders, and she's so positive. Her perfume reminds of me of an old girlfriend waking me from an afternoon nap by kissing me: all flowers. Professionally, Linda isn't obligated to be so positive toward me. I'm falling in love with an old woman here.

"Oh they all say they were the biggest and the best," she says, joking again.

"Why do you criticize me, Linda? Most of the people here are bourgie ex-civil slaves."

"Not criticizing. Flirting. You challenge me."

Bach's *Toccata and Fugue in D minor* helps the river flow outside my window.

I'm in my room sitting and looking out at the river. Linda is wearing a purple sweater, which shows a lovely outline. She emerges into my field of view from the hallway. Where else is she to emerge from? The room exists because of the hallway: the hallway exists because death is part of life. My vision of the hallway exists because my eyes exist. My eyes exist because I am alive. Analytical moments like this make me happy. Happiness is when the sad memories are suppressed. Sad memories can have no hold in the correctly treated chemical mind. Sad memories for killing all those innocent people who did nothing to deserve it. These sad memories become SS memories: Super Sadder memories for the two donkeys that got killed near Paris—where the French had set up a nineteenth-century mock Arab village with whites dressed as Arabs doing Arab things like calculating the sale of dates with abacuses. In the newspaper, the French officials very intentionally said that the donkeys were from the Quresh region of Saudia Arabia. So we had to. And we did. Ah sadness, the mind, and the utterly innocent donkeys, whose heads merged together during the flash and bang. I had the donkeys respectfully buried. I mean *in my mind* I had the donkeys buried with full Islamic honours. The mind only exists due to chemicals one could argue.

What I have before me right at this moment are chemicals, the view of the River Ravi from Pierrefonds, all chemicals. Sure, it's all motion and something, but didn't one of the big scientists change motions and something with chemicals and something? Isn't the word *something* in its print incarnation made out of chemicals? I'm having one of those days when one thing is part of another thing. Circle after circle on the first day of taking new pills. And then on the second day: I see a clear blue day with stark clarity until the satellites come home. However, there is a super rush for four hours after taking the pills: the compartments within my mind generate walls and then almost suddenly I have a history of myself. Here's when I did this: day number, year number; and here's when I did that; day number, year number; so on and so forth.

I've made this mistake before somewhere. At once, I initiate things: "Tatjana Lucrece has gobs of money rotting in the bank; rotting like the last piece of pepper steak and Brussels sprouts the embalmer takes out. She has a drop-dead beautiful daughter."

Linda says: "You shouldn't be talking about embalmers. And why are you thinking of her daughter?"

"All looks. No brains for the market, that's what she says. That's what her mother says."

Linda sets a tray of food down on a small table. "I saw her daughter and spoke with her. Not all a waste —very intelligent, I thought. She does visit regularly, does she? Is that the impression you got?"

Sunday. Visitors' day at the Zoo—a zoo in which the animals are cared for by the same animals who are slightly younger animals of some kind. There is an exchange of money for this service. I look at the vegetables on the plate. I say to myself, I wouldn't wipe Tatjana

Lucrece's arse with them. Something happened to her the other day, and guess what? A young nurse had to wipe her arse. Nothing replaces the pleasure of having your arse wiped by a young visible minority nurse who can't get a job elsewhere due to his or her race. Ah, the pleasure of getting old. Guess who told me? Prejudicial shit, pardon the pun, again.

Dinner is over, the plates and cutlery are being cluttered away. The hallway is now filled with a river of oldies on walkers, wheelchairs, all off to the garden to sit in the sunshine—under sun-blocking umbrellas. Some wait for visiting sons and daughters. How can we have sunshine after supper? It must be summer.

Here I am again in one of my confused out-loud monologues. Linda isn't supposed to hear them, but does because I'm saying them into my recorder. Politely, she notices me noticing her.

I turn to Linda, she expresses no surprise. We've become close. "Professionally, you aren't obligated to be so positive," I tell her, even though she's not really the one I'm drifting into love with. I say thank you, knowing that I may be the caring, highly-educated father she may fantasize about. She, of course, knows that her fantasizing must fade. It is impossible to see a father or a mother in every near-pearly-gater in this last stop before ending up as subatomic particles to be judged and reconfigured by God and then spewed out of a galaxy-producing nursery, galaxies somewhere out there in Hubbleland. I tell her all this and she laughs. I hide nothing from Linda. She knows it's all airless drama.

Hours later, the drama evolves in my head despite

being too old to be a terrorist. Brothers and sisters it's five in the morning: I can't sleep because I've a tactical odour in my mind. Odour? Tactical? How? If a particular odour is coupled with a precise time when that odour is presented to the public it becomes tactical. The odour that I'm familiar with is urine—Noachian loads of it—but we couldn't use urine to cause terror. Partially, our Wahhabis connections paid for the smell of piss which is always near our noses; but I'm dreaming of a different smell, different from the gases used in 1915.

Still in my pyjamas, I confidently and slowly walk past the rooms with different numbers on their doors. I perform cumulative sums of the numbers on the doors and squeeze that sum through the function $\psi \mid x \mid$ to determine at the exact time our Mohammads will do the acts I've designed. This rewarding mental activity leads me to the time when the events will happen. They will happen at 08:13. These events did happen. It's all there, not in black and white, as in the old days, but in zeros and ones. Am I boasting unwarrantedly? Aging non-state actors like me never put on airs. Even when we get old we think in rational blocks producing action and balance. Sure, some of us in our youth owned houses with swimming pools in Palestine, and champagne made in the holy city Karachi; of course, the champagne smelt of urine mixed with Egyptian donkeys and camel skins from Bohri Bazaar.

As early morning light falls on the hallway floors, I walk along to Anver's room and knock on his door. He's sleeping lightly, he always does. The slightest noise or sliver of light wakes him. After knocking, I open the door. A knife-like line of light from the hallway falls on his face.

"Anver, are you awake? Can you listen to my idea for further justice." Now, he's as alert as the ethnic nationalist French-Canadian birds outside. I say: "In a few minutes, can you please call the rest of them here so we can organize a simple event in the Montreal metro and the Toronto subway? Call Muhammad, Muhammed, Mohamed, Mohammad, and white-skinned and blue-eyed Muhameti."

These men are ever so slightly younger than us and are here living with us as false oldies in case something happens. They don't need any equipment at all, just 1.5-litre containers for gasoline each.

I look at Anver and say: "I'm sick of getting old. This aging process makes me want to conduct vitrification against the people who conduct imperialism. My memory is better than what it used to be. This is due entirely to the memory pills. I get nostalgic, I think we need to do something as a parting gift."

Anver says: "Who's parting? I'm in good health. What should I tell our Mohammads?"

"Tell them we have thought up something that will put two cities into a state of panic and there'll be a real loss of money, but not people—that, of course will come later. People can't get to work, this will cost both cities lots of money."

"What do you have in mind?"

"Oh, it's modest and super cheap; we'll not have to ask for supplies at all. What'll we'll need are a few litres of gasoline. I'm planning to spend only a few dollars and it'll all be done with gasoline which the collective Mohammads can buy anywhere."

"But cars don't use gasoline anymore. Everything is electric. No gas," Anver says.

"Mistake. There was a period in our recent history which had people using electric cars but some drivers went back to gas. In fact, more than seventy-five percent went back to gasoline. Also, most terrorism heats things up. Vitrification happens at –135 C—so of course we can see this as methodological meliorism over hot terrorism. Sure, they'd be dead but not blown apart—just frozen to death. Freezing them to death would cost more than all the oil in Saudi Arabia. It would be fun to freeze the royal family to death in the hottest part of the world."

Anver says: "We've been here that long? I know we came ages ago thinking that no one would look for us here. Joseph, when on earth did we move in here? Yeah, sure we can get some gasoline. How are you going to use it? It's not super explosive you know."

We came to see the Toronto subway where there is an x, y axis with some extensions at the eastern end of their subway lines. This breaks the symmetry a wee bit but Torontonians have the Yonge and Bloor lines which run under the city. How are we, men and women in our seventies and eighties, to do high terrorism when only young people can do it? And which underground system do we hit?

We organized it with about six or so litres of gasoline which we purchased from somewhere—it was still possible to buy gas in this early-mid-century.

"What can we do with petrol?" Anver asks.

From flexible plastic sacs they'll wear, they spill gasoline on the various platforms at the Toronto Finch station and the Montreal station Montmorency. The same odour at Kennedy and Honoré Beaugrand. And Berri UQAM-Bloor-Yonge and Kipling-Angrignon; followed by the time-odour complex of Shia Benzine Pars at Snowdon and Saint-Michel.

"This will not hurt anyone. We'll have our people empty a litre and a half of gasoline at each end of the metro system as well as some gas in the centre at Yonge and Bloor. The spills will have to be done within a nanosecond of each other. The exact time connected with the exact smell will make the imperialists listen. It's the least we can do. We aren't going to live forever. That we do this at the exact time and with the same smell will convert into a threat, showing our skills. Further action will be implied by this act, but we'll stay quiet and hope the younger ones will convert the smell to other acts. The smell will be read by the youth to act now. Act now. The older generation is dying off."

Anver says: "If we spill in Montreal and Toronto at the same time—you say 08:13 in both places—they will close down the transportation system. And, it'll be normal Hollywood for them to think that Islamics will be sending flaming subways trains hurtling non-stop through stations. Both Torontonians and Montrealers will see burning trains with screaming passengers converting into charcoal, pressed up against windows, speeding through the Yonge and Bloor station, through Finch station, through Kipling station and burrowing through the Canadian earth, under Kingston to violently emerge in

Montreal's Berri UQAM. Flames to high heaven. We'll fill the entire two metro systems with flaming subway trains speeding through stations."

"Anver, nothing like that at all. No one will be killed. We want to show the West that we can be inventive and not as cruel as they've been. They'll close down the transportation in both cities, costing them millions of dollars."

Anver says: "Why don't we do a worthless peaceful demonstration with placards? This doesn't sound like anything classical: not hot, not cold, polite as a Sunday don't you think?"

"We should bomb the Great Barrier Reef—not so Sundayish is it? And the human count would be low. Truth be told, we sunk drums with explosives onto the reefs and powered the cute little colours."

22

Dairy Queen

I think polite people are ugly. Even if they are not ugly, they become ugly. Their politeness makes their faces wrinkle, their testicles hang, their breasts sag in evacuated pink sacs, thrombotic veins like on the legs of a camel. But this recollection is not about someone polite. This recollection is about a woman I knew. She lived in the Plateau-Mont-Royal area of Montreal in an apartment on Hutchison where the Greek Orthodox church meets the Dairy Queen.

Usha. Now dead. Now alive. Now standing in a claw-foot bath surrounded by red shower curtains, water falling all over her face, which is no longer covered with the taut olive skin that once graced her facial bones. Showers are always moments of great pleasure for her. Tantamount to the excitement of world football. There's flirtation in those poignant hazel eyes: her spotted wrinkled hand palms the frizzy luminous hair out of her eyes. It's grey, not black. Her grey white breasts sag like fried eggs attached to her collar bone with blue veins.

Voices emerge from the ice cream eaters at the Dairy Queen outside. She washes her vagina; the lips too have extended in wave-like folds, and they droop like my balls. But they are not sad. From the bathroom window

I see the Greek Orthodox priest in his black robe walking away from the DQ with a banana split in his hands.

The soap suds of the aged are gentler than the brutally brushed-on soap of the young. Her furrows multiply in the landscape of drooping skin. She puts lots of cream on her feet—if she doesn't they become so dry that they look like the Rubia El Khali.

I've walked into the bathroom to watch you bathe, to watch one particular bead of water follow a predetermined stream to the hole in the bottom of the tub. The hole where all existence goes. The suds of the dead or near-dead are modified in the guts of the living. On the undertaker's table bits of insides are washed down a similar hole.

"Why and how did we get here?" I ask you. I ask you in my memory of you—I mean as I sit here in front of nurse Linda.

"Pass me the soap and stop asking the big questions all the time," you reply, smiling. Linda says: "Pass me the soap—who is asking you to pass the soap. Who's inside your head today. Joseph, who is there?"

I ignore Linda's question and fall back into an old girlfriend's life.

Your hair is still dense and is captured in a white shade of grey. The skin on your arms now hangs like fins. I slowly rub soap on them. You make cooing sounds. Yes, my little one I am soaping you. I give birth to gentle old folks' lather. Your mouth is softened by removed dentures. Slowly, you turn toward the water; the suds wash away.

"I like your fins, are you becoming a fish?" I ask, touching her flesh under her arms.

"I'm becoming a fish, yes, you're becoming a fish," she

says, putting her arms around me. She holds me. I love her. My shirt is wet with her water. I drape a long white towel around her shoulders. She reaches for her glasses. It's been decades since I had a black hair on my body.

23

Schnittke, Stravinsky

Jean is the cook with whom I've become friends. Old Europe, for Jean, means high culture. Saint Martin-in-the-Fields with airborne cooks, pots, pans, cauldrons, and spatula falling on the concrete kitchen floor making a musical noise like the *William Tell Overture*. Because of his class or ethnic background—one hundred percent French-Canadian, farmer father—he is unable to appreciate the jagged, urban, wood-winds-used-as-metallically-percussive instrumental complexities of Igor Stravinsky. Ethnic background has nothing to do with his dislike of the early modern ones. He told me a few days ago that Stravinsky was deeply connected with the church. He's read the CD cover notes. Yes, that fact had slipped my mind; Stravinsky and I are old pals. How could anyone so modern harken back to the dirty church? What inspiration could such a pre-rational institution give him? There are, precisely, no answers.

But the music is irrational, it does not refer to birds in a field, a pending thunder storm, a small bird in the Russian countryside, a prattling brook. Stravinsky's music is like placing some kind of separate boxes of sound beside one another in a large muffin tray and changing their positions so different sound combinations appear.

I'm English upper class, went to public terrorist school without ever getting sexually molested—that was an accomplishment for the nineteen-fifties: laugh if you want to. I lived for ages in an airport. The teachers did not prey on me, nor did my fellow students. For England, that's a feat. I ask Jean what he thinks about Elgar: does he think about rain when he listens to composers?

Jean and I go for a drive in the country. I can see raindrops washing the leaves clean of the raised dust. Due to bumps in the road, we slow down to walking speed. The hot August bush hums with insects and birds. A flock of yellow finches in the dense wall of evergreens gives us momentary glimpses of long, cool lakes. I can hear pebbles being crushed under the tires; then, when the small road becomes asphalt once again, Jean changes to third gear. The walls of bleached wood side barns lean inward toward each other. I see roadside vegetable stalls.

"Stop, I want to buy some fruit and veggies." He pulls over on the side of the road, and lights a cigarette. A few cars zip by. A dozen corn cobs for two dollars and fifty cents; a bag of cucumbers, one dollar and fifty cents; squash for even cheaper. Country fruit stalls evolve into the large supermarkets as we pass a few medium-sized towns. Here, far from Montreal, these supermarkets have various spices for making curries; fresh coriander—which no true Orientalist can live without—things that one would never have dreamed of getting a few years ago. Fat farmers with salt-of-the-earth hands sell tomatoes mixed with the genes of white rhinos. The seller hands me what I have paid for in a plastic bag made from oil of Saudi Arabia. "D'autre chose, monsieur?" Yes, more white rhino, less Saudi Arabia in my tomatoes if you please. "No thank you," I say with a smile. We never used the air conditioning. Pro-environmental types we are.

We're back to another small road. Jean turns to the left, avoiding potholed passages. Trees, thinking that the road is a river, cower as if to drink through the eddies of dust our car makes. The windy wake leadeth them to still waters, and, with optimism, the low branches recoil back to their loftier positions. More rain is imminent, and we have ample proof that a fox must be getting married, because the sun is shining at the same time that it is raining.

The subject now has become classical music. "People who haven't any training in classical music tend to try to pass judgments of one kind or another. Why try to guess who composed it? You want to make yourself sound cultured, educated and sensitive?"

"I just like it," he confidently replies, adding: "Push the lighter in for me, will you." We're good enough friends to have an argument.

"If you just enjoy it, then why do you have to let me know that you're oh-just-so-curious about, what, when, and who composed it?" I had no idea that rural Quebec had such a vast network of roads with so many turns. "This isn't a highway? Why is every road named after a saint?"

The mood has changed, and it's all my fault. Jean thinks that I am trying to annoy him. I subject him to further opprobrium: "Why can't you simply keep the questions about who and when composed whatever inside you? Why try to indirectly embarrass me by saying: 'Look, you don't know.' Why not go to the library one day and spend a few hours about who, what, baroque or not baroque, atonal or not atonal, modern or not so modern, plainsong or not plainsong? The learning experience would satisfy you. But no, you have to try to be cultured about it. You have to let others know that you know about classical music, even if it's an awfully tiny little bit. Whoopee shit. So you can name a few composers—the most obvious ones—wow can you really tell the difference between Mozart, Paganini and Schnittke? Holy shit, this makes you an expert on classical music. Thing is, you don't know the first thing about music technically. Certainly nothing about it historically. So what's the point in name dropping? Does this represent culture for you? Bucolic curiosity makes you cultured. Yes of course that will make you look highly cultural in the French-Canadian world."

"You're making it impossible to have a discussion with you. Why are you like this today?"

His old black car of Germanic extraction moves down kilometres of gravel road.

"Mean? About a truth? What truth were you're going to utter?"

"Your attacks say nothing to me; they don't expose my character flaw, but yours. All you want is to hate and embarrass me. That's it, isn't it?"

He lights another cigarette. "That's the truth about your real intentions isn't it? Admit it. You see nothing nice in me. I am all pretentiousness, simple-minded—admit that's all you see in me. I'm always nice and generous with you."

As the car moves on, more self-deluded trees lap up

water. A splendid pewter-coloured lake tilts in the horizon as we turn. My homily continues: "Yes, I admit I'm fond of invective. Nothing wrong with that when truth is concerned. Invective produces truth. Politeness hides the truth. You haven't any real interest in anything except for Hollywood banalities, and even there it's just so you can say that you've seen it."

"Should I leave real ideas to intellectuals such as you? Why are you hitting me like this? I am Jean, your cook. You opened my world a little and now you're hitting me."

"Yes, Jean, you're right. A pusillanimous thinker such as you can't really hurt me back, can you?" Whoops, I can see the tears? Whoopsy, he's crying now.

"You're a one-dimensional cook."

"I am not crying." He has a tremor in his voice.

"Now what are your interests? Gardening? Bad cooking? Non-newsworthy news? Phoning your mother? Soliciting your father's views on politics. So learned that twenty black ants could carry all his ideas for twenty years." He's fully in tears now. I bring a unencompassable rationality to his thinking. And he'll win because, in the end, I'll have to apologize before we get back to the home. He's the servant I've beaten. I offer to light him a cigarette: that'll calm him. Mustn't get to the tears, not quite, not now.

The conversation has hidden the fact of indicator lights blinking on and off in sync with the light on the dashboard. Click, then the dashboard light, click, then the dashboard light, click, then the dashboard light.

"Turn the indicator off for fuck's sake, are you turning or what?"

Providentially, more rain begins to fall in fat drops on the windscreen. My memory of Damascus fades into a long lake. He closes the sun roof. God replaces his tears with rain. Allegorical afternoon we're having. Music, composers, rain, tears, no tears. Smoke, more smoke. Our conversation is unending. I say I'm sorry. He says ok, no problem, but I feel like a bit more argument, just to keep me in shape.

Linda's at the routine task of taking my blood pressure. She has on fox bladder perfume.

"Linda, tell me where you were born, I don't know a thing about you."

She's wearing a long black dress with a V-neck today. She's tanned because she just came back from a Caribbean vacation.

"Well then, if you can't tell me about yourself, can you tell how your vacation was? Who did you go with? Where did you go?"

"I went with a friend."

"Male or female? Female until midnight?" I ask.

Silence.

"I see. No information, I see."

"I was born right here in Montreal."

"You deserve better."

"Joseph, that's a very biased remark, isn't it?"

"Suppose it is. Suppose it is."

"Get into trouble in the slave-dominated Caribbean?"

"What could you possibly mean by that?"

"What do I possibly mean by that?" I repeat into her nice face. "What is it about me that you find ..."

"I know you were accused of something very bad … maybe murder, but you were …"

"It was thrown out of court. No proof."

"I know you're innocent. But you did arrange it all, didn't you?"

"You see, you're falling in love with me. Yes, I arranged it all."

"How did that happen? What did you do?"

"I love it when you ask for details." I point my hand to birds on a tree on the snowy lawn.

Nurse Linda admits that she did some research on the issue of the codex. She must have been reading my diary, or someone told her something.

"That's about it. And now there's some new evidence."

"Are you ever going to talk to these detectives?"

"Haven't I just done exactly that?"

24

Strait of Hormuz, Bernadette Aodhfionn

I dream that Usha, dressed in a black skirt and white shirt, waits for me to arrive. She's the same age as when I met her, north of 77 and thin. She's at the airport and she's back to smoking. In the distance, she sees the arrival and departure announcement board. She is nervous. It has been ages since she has seen me. A red line under a certain flight announcement flashes "arrived." I walk down to arrivals so she won't have to see me from the observation café. She is excited despite the funeral she has to face tomorrow. She is coming to the home to live. Is that what is happening, am I picking her up so she can live with us?

For some strange reason, she's late coming out of arrivals. Why? They have nothing on her. They have nothing on me. The authorities always arrest the wrong Islamics. They supplied us with the explosives—they got that right. Open the bodies—you'll see the traces of steak and kidney pie explosives—they didn't do that. They arrested a few Moslems from working-class backgrounds. As usual. Stupid cunts. What are they asking her? Where were you on the morning of such and such a terror date? Who are you to ask? On the morning of the events of London Bridge, I was in Iran—advising them on how to block the Strait of Hormuz, how to hit Israel; how to admit that the Palestinians are over. And, now the project is to stop the Jewish State from taking over Islamabad. The Palestinians no longer matter. They are cannon fodder. Well, Mr. Canadian-Immigration-officer-working-to-keep-Jews-happy: I was in Bloomsbury performing Moslem blowjobs on a corpse while my Islamic friends pull jewellery—rings and necklaces—off the dead and deadish heavenish.

I continue waiting for her to come out of arrivals. Christ, they are not questioning her, are they? I remember my training in terror central. Stay cool. Never move too fast. I imagine her within transit walking from McDonald's to a bookstore; then back again to a transit bar; chatting with the woman working in the bar; chatting with the staff working at various ticket counters. She is walking slowly throughout Trudeau International. She is now staring at the Zionist Air Lines counter. She shows her landing card to the uniformed white French-Canadian nigger. White nigger nods. I'm too old to do anything anyway. And yes, I balanced all those people in Bloomsbury. What are you going to do about it? Up your arse—you piece of intentionally uneducated white shit. What gives these bastards the right to ask a world citizen questions about how long she will be staying here and if she has a medical plan or not. Now fuck off and let her into Canada so I can die in Pierrefonds with my terrorist friends. If you don't let me in, I promise I'll inspire the next generation, and this inspiration will make sure that your city's ambulance workers will have job security for the next five centuries.

These thoughts erode in the airport air. She's cleared immigration—the doors swing open. Perfunctorily, we hug. Escalators down to the parking lot. As we drive away, we see the open undercarriages of landing airplanes. Our faces inside the car are in darkness; slowly, facial details emerge as street lights and cars go by, we put things back together but not by talking about our projects. I can't for the life of me remember the conversation we had. It was the same-old same-old stuff; there was nothing new. Did we chat about the few Abduls who were our masters? Not at all. Did we have a significant number of white intellectuals with us? One or two, but significant. Lips traced in red lipstick, her left hand is on the steering wheel while her right hand neatly flicks ashes into tray. I'm a little rounder for the years, but a physically strong old man.

A large colourful laser highway sign flutters past in the night sky, a few ad-halos also flash by. But these are near-dream-near-accurate descriptions, so anything goes. I wonder why she has set the car computer to read road signs? She turns it off, and we now see only the few holo road signs. McDonald's has been engaged in a long legal battle to protest the state's demand that it remove all its holographic adverts and replace them with optional signs. Since the sign law, the night sky has become visible and many people go for short star-watching romps on the highways.

As Usha and I get closer to Pierrefonds, bright yellow sodium lights obliterate the calm. This is in my recent past: I'm picking her up at Trudeau Airport to bring her to live with all her old friends.

"Good, you've come to Montreal. Thanks for all those postcards. Did you give up your apartment in London? Your money holding out?"

"Yes, money all ok—and I have enough to pay the home. Thanks for inviting me to live with you."

I look towards her with ancient excitement. I tell her: "I need your friendship. Very much. Faraway places we went to. What do you remember the most?"

"Mostly your wonderful leadership." She is smiling. Road signs flutter past.

The compartments in my mind flutter to clarity like an old airport announcement board. Must be the pills I took this afternoon. I remember once when I met Usha in a hotel in country X. My hand touches elevator button forty-five. Our eardrums pop as the mirrored, carpeted box hushes upwards. We step out of the elevator and I notice an empty hallway; her coat rustles against her purse. We are doing a job in an easy Canadian city with tons of snow. The door clicks open. A large picture-window frames skyscrapers breathing out white woolly steam into the freezing winter night. The bright rotating landing pad lights make the steam glow. We drink wine, and after a while, the city lights in the tall buildings extinguish in unified blocks: first, the lights of an entire floor of a bank building; then a few more at the extreme west end of a building a few kilometres away; then, all in one blink the lights of a building directly across from us. The city falls into a coma for a few hours and wakes up to one of our operations. Through the windows, we see an ambulance glide by on the street below. For fun,

I open the window and a gush of cold wind enters the room; we hear a low-decibel phhut-phhut of a police helicopter crossing the city; its trailing silhouette falling on some of the lit windows. I put my arm around her to protect her from the cold. We kiss for a long time. Did we really kiss? She looks out at the uneventful city. "Light pollution coming to an end tonight I see ... ah, maybe now we'll be able to see the stars?"

25

The milk of human kindness

My head turns away from the window in an afternoon on a particular Sunday, seven days exactly before my birthday. A bright blue car passes, then a roundish brown one. Never much traffic outside. My grey hair, like the tail end of galactic spiral arm, follows my head, which turns again toward the window. From the hall comes a persistent smell of urine mixed with floor-cleaning products.

A nurse—in white this time. Nurses don't wear uniforms anymore—so why's this one in white? Must be because of a medical emergency of some kind or another. Yes, I see that Mrs. Gandal in room 215 has a transparent tube in her arm and that she is lying down, eyes closed.

"How's she doing?"

The doctor is wearing a tweed jacket. "She'll be fine. You're a friend?" I look at him thinking: Why keep her alive? Give you a paycheque? What else are you going to do with your life?

"Well, yes, I know her a little, not too much. Is she going to be alright?'

"We should give this a bit more time."

I look directly at the tube. I show him that I am looking at the tube.

"Oh, don't worry about that, she's getting some sleep now." The tube is attached to a machine with LEDs in all colours, which tick, tick, tick away.

¬ I tell Nurse Linda about a woman. I'm friends with the wife of a dead man, you see. This makes her smile: her pink lips lift into her multiracial face. She presents me with the pills. Imagine, I say in my when-I-was-your-age tone. I am trying to impress her with my vast knowledge: Imagine trying to impress a dead banker's wife, here in this last stop before paradise, with the economic details of why Mohammed (PBUH) moved from Mecca to Medina. She doesn't know Muhammad, she doesn't know Mecca, and Medina was a little shop were she would sometimes shop before the *zamana* of the old folks home.

I get a flutter when I see Tatjana. Linda bids me an unprofessional "Bye until the next time," which will be for my four o'clock or whatever o'clock. I must take the pills because I don't have an illness. Memory is an illness.

Well, then what am I dying of? Tatjana's slender hand reaches for the door knob. I am not lonely. I have my thoughts: She is seventy-ish, somewhat mannish, and waves to cars. No chance of DNA repair capability even if they try enzyme telomerase. We have a patient who is suffering from dyskeratosis congenita with telomeres out of whack, I suppose. I don't mean to imply anything about her mental processes, which are sound. But I've never really liked sound women, have I? Linda is not around to listen to this. Just as well. Over-disclosure destroys even the most patient of nurses, even the ones born on the theatrical stage of the milk of human kindness, I suppose. I'm not one to be too demanding: I'd be scared to push her away from me.

I visit Tatjana. The name sign on her door reads: Tatjana Lucrece, dead-banker's wife, now living in impressionistic-medico-uric splendour, beside a river, next to Arles if you'll have it, and she'll have it because it does not really matter—because she can't tell the difference between Picasso and a photograph of a wriggle-de-piggedly car accident on the front page of a newspaper. Today's papers are ever so light, and not transparent. She has a drop-dead beautiful daughter of some worth.

Was the daughter ever a student of Islam? Keep away from uneducated dead bankers' wives, I keep telling myself. But whom will I talk to then? Why should I discuss Islam with her? What should I discuss with her? Am I giving her a prior-to-perhaps-purgatory course in Islam before she visits her heathen's heaven?

It's another day: Tatjana has slippered off along the west hallway.

Yesterday, when we were in her room, she held up a toothbrush and asked: "What's this for? It looks so familiar, but I can't remember what I used it for. Tell me. And please, please don't tell anyone I asked you."

26

Panther's claw

Winters have drifted by. She touched my hand. She remembers what happened a few nights ago. I wandered over to her room late at night. No, that was last month. Perhaps nothing has drifted by. A buzzing fly just shot by. What sort of noise does a DNA chain make when it replicates for the last time? What sort of noise does it make when it is not replicating? Experimental gerontology. What could a last time possibly mean? Are we aware that it is replicating for the last time? Do we know about this final replication because researchers know that DNA command central is saying ok cell, go fuck off, it's all over? No, that is not what happens. Here's what happens: the research shows that a final anti-replication command is given because research strongly suggests that this kind of command ought to take place given that all previous research has established that this ought to be the case. When we become conscious of precedent, we become conscious of something we are not yet fully conscious of, we understand things only partially. But you see when the young researcher is looking at a past experiment, he is looking at it in continuous time—what the fuck does all that mean? Face the fact that the researcher—and they are mostly men still, even after so many years of changes in other fields, including terrorism—is looking at the past in a partial future. As we age, the past fades, like passing mustard fields seen from a train moving from Marseille to Adge. I see distinct parts of the corner of a wall where I as a child buried a bottle with a note inside. It was a rainy day. Black macintosh. A father at work. I'm to make the coal fire in a little house outside London.

Or Tatjana is near me or has just walked past me. Tatjana's a bit sunny, not stupid: she laughs at my political jokes so she can't be stupid. They have made her memory much better. She adds a little something to the place where we come to kick the bucket. She sits in a red leather armchair beside the big window. We sit together and watch the black river move. My hand almost touching hers.

I disclose all this to Linda. I give her all the details. If I give her all the details, then this disclosure will drive her closer to me; she's young and she'll become my personal friend. Ah! To have a young friend. What a joy it is to have a mind that operates at such a different speed and with a cataloguing system that is so much clearer than mine. My narration of Usha's (or was it Tatjana's or was it Jean's?) crying works. Linda invites me to her house. That's what life is about—attracting people to my somewhat ugly being. Who says I'm ugly? They've done terrible things—much worse than poor little me. What they did, however, was not for free. They were dead. I'll be dead. Linda will age, and she'll forget me. She has no options. Her cells will delete me from her memory before she dies. She will die a few years after my departure. What's the point of having a memory when in a few decades the brain's circuitry snaps soundlessly like a spider web torn by a panther's claw? Was my fight for higher morals worth it?

27

Calendar

Muḥarram
Ṣafar
Rabīʿ al-Thānī
Jumādā al-Ūlā
Rajab
Shaʿbān
Ramaḍān
Shawwāl
Dhū al-Qaʿda
Dhū al-Ḥijja

We always needed money for operations, and we always had to save a bit from one operation to the next, because we had to have money for air tickets to go see people for project money. The process was like getting a grant for a university department. The sound of low-flying airplanes coming in from Europe to Pierre Elliot Trudeau International takes me back to a zamana when I spent lots of time in airports. From the window of the aircraft, I see eight-hundred-metre buildings shaped like bananas made of steel and glass, standing in sand. As the plane moves nearer the ground, I think, all that glass was once sand. The thought vanishes when I hear an abrupt screech as the undercarriage melts into the hot runway. I notice that the rabbi who is wearing a shtreimel and has blonde locks running down the sides of his head can no longer read *The Jerusalem Post* jiggling in front of his eyes: I smile inside. Iqbal once told me that no rabbi lands in a place like Dubai. Walking down the steps, I inhale deeply. There must be a living sea somewhere nearby. Air time, dark green vegetation, cadmium sand, and jet exhaust produce jet lag. Remove from the journey these four things but keep the dark green vegetation, sand and jet exhaust and I'll still to this day get jet lag. What I have now at this very moment is externally triggered de-synchronicity. Can we use de-synchronicity to get more funding? We had to come up with new things to get the money, just like any other job.

Is it impossible to use time itself as a terrorist instrument? Say we did a time related event: what would those extreme and unconditional friends of country X be saying on CNN? How did these terrorists use the forth dimension to subject innocent people to terrorism? What actually was it—what did they do? What did the Arabs do with time to hurt us so badly? How can we prevent this from happening again? They might establish a Home Time Security Agency to prevent us from doing it again. All we did to the Americans was to reset the clocks in banks and other state institutions such as airports and military bases to metric time. The retards couldn't find a way out until someone—a scientist with a Jewish-sounding name like Smith used his knowledge of an inflationary universe to adjust Americans to another system. To our credit, the total damage was impressive. One million people who were airborne at the time in various airplanes all died due to measurement errors: tons and tons of planes crashing into runways, seas, oceans and lakes, Walmarts; many planes crashing into each other, producing firecracker colours; hundreds of surface and underground train "accidents." Not to mention problems at hospitals: total light failure in operating rooms—500,000 (approximately) patients died painfully. We Moslems inflicted great pain on America by changing the measure of time.

I'm mentioning a series of events to whom? Am I talking with Iqbal, who has no hair, or to Anver, who has decided to dye his hair black these days? Here, in sequence, are the events: imperial contact; colonialism, resistance, social decay, departure, rebirth, self-knowledge, oceans, ships, seas, clouds over rivers, life as an emergent hermaphrodite (*khusra*) in Sialkot (s/he was not part of our unit but met us a few times); life as a kid in Zamalik; seeing black and white television for the first time; shirts made in Manchester; and then resistance within. And then Bang. Resistance equals bang, which is now boring. Western democracies were not the only ones getting bored with conventional B. B works wonderfully, but we now want a renaissance: Brothers, I would tell my unit (excluding Ms Sialkot), brothers, we must to yannie, hit the golden age of terrorism. No more R = B. Of course: it's still B that we are aiming for. But how to make a B that will have them reeling for a decade? Only Allah could help us. Of course, we full well know only numbers will help us. Allah is a zero, and zero is his messenger, the other side might be thinking. The rank-and-file did the smaller things that Islam might or might not have made them do.

We believe the white police at the command of the Jew did most of it, someone in another cell said.

Imran Smith asks: "What about the King David Hotel? Who did that?"

Another unit member, Said, answers: "What was the King David Hotel? Some of us have a far vaster canvas to correct the wrongs, and correcting the wrongs does not mean using mild political objects like social democracy or an easy-to-get nuke, or an easy-to-organize demo. Any old agent can get a nuke, go to Kiev and take a right down the main street, continue for ten minutes and knock on the blue door. A man with a blonde beard will serve you—take a number. Nukes—what a joke. Keep reading—I'll take you far from the madding crowd into the world of super-T without R = B. "T" is not time in the Newtonian sense, but T = Terror-Time. The chap who did our numbers told us something utterly meaningless: T and T are complex conjugates of each other. We snickered into our *kafiyas* and the discussion shifted to something less complex.

At any rate, all they have to offer is Risk = threat x vulnerability x consequence.

Why did I do this thinking and all this travelling and glad-handing for supplies and money? Well, it was not simply to get justice in the world, as the naive left in the West thinks: I did it all to get admiration from Jews. There were women in our unit, not the cover-up lower-class types (who got raped once in a while, but not by anyone in our units) but ones with the same colour hair as the rabbi on the flight to somewhere that felt like Bishkek: Bishkek, where we believe our future lies.

We would ask ourselves, what is it that we *can't* use as an instrument of retaliation? We talk until the Wee Willie Winkie non-hours. Sure, we can use trains, boats, buildings, and old-fashioned passenger aircrafts, but we're now thinking about making righteous retaliations that would be as important as a scientific revolution, leaving old Newton dead at Westminster—forty Euros to visit his grave. Can we use jet lag to screw the West, someone would joke? There is jet lag up there now—750,000 to one million people airborne every nanosecond of human existence. Surely, we can use figures like this to tell you: please stop the pillage, if you don't, we will Islamo-time-machinecide you in the cunt. Tons of emergent jet lag to exploit. Can we produce permanent jet lag if we do B? But why return to smelly old B? I simply don't like all the nails we have to stuff in the package: I do have some moral standards. How can we get all the planes currently airborne into permanent jet lag? We were inventing the El Alan Turing Terror Machine. Endless discussions in our little home near Hayes and Harlington.

Some people like to save whales from the Japanese, but I would like donkeys to survive our struggle for human liberation. I had badges made for our unit: "I heart symbol Donkeys." A donkey was never killed in any operation I governed, and I organized many operations in Islamic lands that were Sialkot-free.

Imran Smith would say we should invent time-based terrorism. Everyone in our unit thought he was loopy. He wasn't loopy at all. Nor was he an agent provocateur. We knew him. Did he mean time without B? He did numbers for us on trains that always move in synchronicity to democracy. During a meeting, someone with an Oxford accent from Peshawar asked if Smith meant that we use time as replacement for the old B? We knew that we had to replace the old means, so on and so forth—they couldn't be used forever, endless chatter in large high-up rooms in seven-star hotels in our many nights in the electrified cities of South Asia and beyond.

More about our funding: I am picked up in the airport lounge. The man with the goatee sitting in front of the steering wheel looks like Usha on a masculine day. The sunlight dazzles off the black car's chrome and back into the atmosphere. The car was recently made by Turks who are the final keepers of the flame of internal combustion and the Caliphate of the twenty-first century. My hand moves across the severely air-conditioned space to shake the manicured hand of Abdul Sincere Abdul, representative of one of three South Asian-Asian countries—take your pick, but not Myanmar. For comic effect, he "Salams-al-lic-cums" me directly in the face with an intentional English accent.

"Joseph, do you have any luggage?" He seems friendly-neutral with me, despite several meetings in small-minded English towns.

"Just this little carry-on. If I do any more shopping, I'll have to shop for a suitcase. Thanks for having me." Smiles, but no further chatter. The driver takes me to where I am staying.

We move along a perimeter highway that Europeans engineered. Thank Allah *they* didn't make the road. An idiotic flag on the antenna flutters regally. My lungs have always been my Achilles heel. Tomorrow, in this home for the unrepentant, I have to go down the hall and then up the elevator to the X-ray department. But now, I am not talking about my last years in this home. Currently, I am telling you about my funding contact. I have a slight case of tight-chested Mercedes-arctic-osis. Lungs have always been my weakness. Massive asthma if I come near cats, dogs, or horses.

Linda comes into the room as I relive this story somewhere in front of my mind. She says hello and looks at some wall-mounted papers connected to my health. My mind says to itself, Anver, are you there? Black-haired Anver. I know Linda has just walked into my room, but my mind is saying Anver. Fellow capital-T terrorist Anver.

I should tell this story to Iqbal, who might have come with me. Bastard is sitting in front of me, while I read to him from my recollections. He's fallen asleep. Why do I keep calling him Iqbal? Is his name Anver? Pills for MIC lead to a multi-framed memoreality. All at the same time. Sometimes I can't take it. Sometimes I cry with the flood of it all coming back to me. I don't mean guilt in any sense at all.

28

Damascus, toothbrush

We are walking to the car parked in the driveway. In the large black Mercedes, we move through a thinly populated part of the city as if Damascus or a city like that ever had a thinly populated part. After winding through smaller and smaller streets, we pull up to a large white villa surrounded by palm trees and birds flying in paths like airplanes. The traffic sounds from the main road fade, but I can still hear planes landing at Trudeau Airport not far from here. Let me get this straight: I am talking about getting funding during the nineteen-eighties, although I now am living sometime in 2040? These pills to fight off early onset hot dogs in the mind are confusing me—memory imbricationosis, as my eighteen-year-old doctor jokes. Are my memories, my goals—all my states—being affected by these pills? Are my levels of guilt adjusting to normal? Of course, I feel guilt. But then I focus on the West. I say, not guilty, not then not now not ever. Now, I thank Allah for the pills, which are letting me fall back into my memory, like a head falling in Saudi Arabia.

I am staying in a place with a large usury-inflected garden. Scarlet flowers jet out of emerald green leaves, and beside this place of botanical beauty stands a very current flower, which is surrounding us with green petals of money. We can, within the programme, do whatever we like with the money. And then, in old age, we will not feel guilty about having blown things up. And people. The money comes like a long electronic snake from there to here, then a bomb goes off and/or an entire section of South Kensington has super-acute dysentery for six weeks. Brown fluid terrorism—yes, that is what the press actually called it. We got part of the English water supply. We send a message: We are responsible for the dysentery. Get your troops out or your Thames will flow brown: the River Ravi at Westminster. We ate ham and cheese sandwiches afterwards; we just had to eat.

Driving around in this city, I swear I saw a Viagra ad beside an equally huge poster of their head of state.

From my two-floors-up window I see two gardeners dressed in worn hand-me-down suits chatting under the shade of a tree. They're having a bucolic conversation, no doubt—I can tell by the way they're moving their hands. On a green hump in the middle of the lawn the size of Delaware, a fountain shoots out a one-millimetre-thin beam of water, rising ten metres and splattering back on a black marble fountain base. The democracy of some people.

I walk downstairs and out toward a waiting car. Naseem, the older one, in a blue *galabaya*, opens the car door. We drive. I see a few donkeys tolerating abuse and carrying heavy bulbous television sets on their backs—they have been carrying these televisions since the time of Christ. I pray for the donkeys and pray to Allah that I will never kill one of these beasts during an operation.

A fat brown palm ushers me up clean marble steps to a room with white walls. Behind thin gauze curtains, French windows give way to a broad patio with a view of another garden the size of the Isle of Man.

I've lost my geography again: I don't know where I am. Am I in the old folks home as an old man or am I the younger man undressing and opening a transparent plastic bag in the bathroom of a hotel in Dushanbe or some similar city in a similar region? It's clear. I'm a young man whose anger has been displaced, rather, by airports, than absorbed in airports. I went to about six million airports, and I lived in one. I was innocent when I actually lived in one for five days. I waited for days for our partners to arrive—they arrive dressed all in black. I am actually innocent now. The imperialists are the guilty ones. The plastic bag reveals razor blades. I lather my face: the razor painlessly and violently moves over my skin. Then I sit down on a white leather armchair (which is not made from shaving lather). In front of the window I meditate on jet lag and how it might be changing the way our brains work. Jet lag always makes me ask myself: Why did I make this long journey? What's this journey I'm making? Why couldn't I have become less familiar with airports?

Effortlessly, my head sinks to one side and then, assertively, I sit up straight: I look into a day dream. I connect the massive Arab eagles flying high above me with jet lag. Eagles. Jet lag. The Syrian eagles ride Zionist thermals in the blue air, which is Jewish air when you think about it. All air has radar bouncing through it. And they're making radar signals which are kosher—radar blessed by a Rabbi: a happy mixture of science and religion. Above me, in all that endless blue, the eagles masterfully twitch their wings for a precision that only they can define, eyes like moles in the sky. I remember the mole on the stewardess's face on the way here. Her mole became the visual centre point for the current trip. Black radial spokes spreading out from her mole are my life and all its directions. All those lines coming from her mole. The pist-pist spitting of water sprinklers outside pulls me out of my genetic indolence. There is someone knocking at the door.

A cold December brings us to a freezing French-Canadian January. Now, a younger version of the Naseem says: "Good afternoon, Docktor Macleod." An Islamic nod means that the man, Funding-us-Underground-Islamicus, has arrived. He is waiting downstairs. I nod and walk down a hall with white carpets. The door clicks shut. My body falls into the routine of dressing up: a clean white shirt, left arm in first, and grey pants. I half Windsor the tie, but then remove it, thinking: formality. I run my white collar over the collar of the blue cotton jacket like an innocent little Iranian in the middle of Terminal E somewhere in Thailand. I walk down the wide wooden steps I walked up earlier in the afternoon. Razor-sharp winter wind rumours were circulating today that my pills are producing good results. Marble old-aged steps. I decided not to take the elevator. It was nothing for a man of my physical condition. I now have on a pink undershirt over a black silk shirt. A regal looking young woman of Italian origin asks me to go in there and show my lungs to her. But before she click-clicks the camera she makes two mole-like dots on my chest with a marker.

I'm walking down the steps. The jet-black ravens caw outside.

Let's see now, where's that place, you know, where we see traces of all different religions all mixed up together? It was a Canaanite religious place, then it was a Greek temple, followed by a Roman one, a Byzantium church, and lastly a mosque with a white table and a cup of Earl Grey tea beside it. Iqbal has a few questions.

Who in hell's name would have thought we'd have ended up in the same old folks home? How could this happen? Oh, my Director of Operations, what were the chances? I hated you. But I now love you. Were you born in Sialkot? Tell me the truth. Are you intentionally confusing me with another Iqbal? But then why are you here if I'm much older than you? You sometimes confuse me with an older man who lives here. He's from Bombay. Oriental confusion?

"The mosque you are describing—aren't you wilfully mistaking our country for another one? I don't get your sense of humour."

"You've always laughed at what I said."

"We have a special guest for you at lunch."

"I don't like surprises in foreign lands."

"What foreign lands are you talking about? You know our language, culture, everything about us et cetera ..."

"... et cetera, et cetera." We laugh.

At the café, overlooking a small mosque, I observe the architectural details: "Look at how well all the different architectural phases are combined into one nearly tolerable whole—now what do you make of it? Can you arrange a trip for us to see this mosque?"

Lunch and inanities. A few guests, all one-time acquaintances of my old influential Me now bid their farewells to Me before the summer heat encourages indolence. I sit in the car, hands on my knees: I am whisked back to the fresh villa. I fall asleep. Usha's son comes tomorrow. He's very tall. Blonde hair. Nordic, not Irish. Wonder if he'll bring me a bottle of boggy scotch or a monochromatic vodka.

The noises of possessive ravens overlap the sweet rising and falling high mass of migratory Bulbuls. The caw-caw of the black priests becomes, a few hours later, a soft persistent knocking at the edge of my sleep. They are taking me back to the airport; along a smooth road, a checkpoint with casual, smoking soldiers loitering in front of a red setting sun. This time, I look at Abdul-or-equivalent behind the steering wheel and firmly assert in a Turkic or equivalent language my right to not have air conditioning. The mullahs with their powerful voices blow all the A380s off the runways up into the thin air, the airport becoming a black spot somewhere in the past.

In the humming cabin, I read the music review section of *The Financial Times*, a light discussion of Aida-on-the-Nile written by Thomas Silver-or-Gold but not Uraniumberg. Hours later, the plane banks over Suez, Port Said, then a stretch of blue water; Cyprus, then more blue water. Below are the Italians—the prime inventors of bonds, banks, formalized money and fraud; the Swiss; and the Gauls with their wonderful, easily adaptable political models for all of Africa. Untraceable electronic deposits have been made into untraceable accounts. Particles function dually as waves and money: money and its electronic friends are not predictable. Well, Iqbal, what did you think of our adventure to get the funding? Iqbal, you came with me. Do you remember? Iqbal hasn't really been paying attention. He's not breathing; in fact he's stopped breathing completely. Can't be. My second dead person in a month. Nurse. Nurse. Pulse. Neck. Wrist. Gone: 14:59, a sunny Tuesday in the month of September. Saddest thing is I'll never know where in my story he died. Iqbal. Mad as a March Hare. He did Russell Square. He did Triangle Below Canal Street and he did Chicago Circle. Two hundred in each geometry. One hundred and fifty-five injured on average: quick, honey, call the ambulances: people need to be saved.

29

El Kairaya-El-Ma'ha'russa

A phone rings. Moronically, I turn to look at it ringing on top of a pile of books. I notice my character change as soon as I hear a "Hello" on the other end.

"Well thanks for all the interest. There is indeed a revival of all this taking place. You're the second person who has contacted me regarding this matter."

He blathers about how nice it is to speak with me, about my publications blah blah.

"That would be possible." Yes, buffoon, a meeting would be possible.

A few days later, we meet at a small restaurant in Montreal. The noisy bastard has, like me, aged. Yes, I pretend that I recognize him.

Despite the steam on the inside of the window panes, sunlight falls through onto our table.

"I'm flattered with all the attention. Thank you, et cetera."

Is Anver doing theatre again with me? I think his Mild Cognitive Impairment is playing games with him or is it late-onset schizophrenia? Pretending he doesn't know me, he says: "Glad to meet you."

I return the compliment: "Pleasure's all mine." I get ready for more banalities. At least I'm not at home among the old ones.

"Have you lived in Montreal for long?" Anver, the refined actor, asks.

I muster a sense of subtlety. "I've been living here for a long time, one could say; from the States and England originally." And without waiting for more inanities, I take the initiative. "I just severely criticized him when it wasn't supposed to be done. Tell me what's wrong with that?"

An original thought enters his head. "People think you organized his abduction." Original, that's what I said.

"There wasn't an abduction—we weren't into authors—we were into Bang Bang and not cultural studies, and we were into burning major art collections. Many think I had a role in it: I'm proud to say that I had a role in exposing this writer. But was there any proof that I had participated other than publishing a negative review that looked at the central issues—is that a crime?"

Then, for charming surprise, I throw a statement—an inductive one, I suppose. "If it isn't, then, you'll have to leave, fuck off. However, I must say that this cloak-and-dagger stuff keeps my brain alive, like learning new computer programmes. Thank you." Remembering that this fuck has come to hear me talk, I, again, take my old man's pause and blurt out in old man's cracked voice: "What's your interest in me?"

"Thought I'd look at things from all sides," Anver says.

"Ah ha. Novel idea." He tries to get a word in but I cut him off. "All sides? you wanted to meet someone who just may be wrongly accused of having maybe planned the murder of a writer?"

"He did disappear. Face this fact."

I continue Anver's theatre. "Thankfully, you admit this." I make another staged pause. "Years ago, I knew someone who looked sort of like you. Different accent. So what if it can be proven that I had planned a murder or kidnapping? A few years in prison before I die. What if I hadn't planned it, but I knew how it was going to be carried out and said nothing to prevent it from happening? What if I had been or am still now an ideological accomplice? Yes, I knew what was going on, because I know this field. There was a plot. I may have known about it. Would I then be guilty for not having warned the police and would I become a prime accomplice? You can't throw a literary critic in jail for doing his job, can you? Malice is mine. I could even make a bit of money if he had been killed, stories to the newspapers and all that—others have done worse, you know—I'd just be a simple opportunist. However nasty it may all seem to the untrained eye."

Linda comes into my room. Anver's words have become small black cows floating in the bright green hills of my mind. Linda leaves. Anver continues.

"Anything about me in the paper? Plans were indeed discovered. And some called from the mosque run by Mohammad M. Mohammad have admitted—admitted? Admitted what? Admitted off the record, don't you mean? But, of course, you know that nothing can be proven, or at least nothing has been proven yet. There was no murder. But that's not the point at all, is it?"

"I just wanted to hear what you'd say about your past," Linda says.

"What if I had been an ideological accomplice only?

And that it can be proven without the shadow of a doubt that I knew of what was going on because of my learning in the field. I knew a case where almost the same thing happened. You're too young to remember; back then I predicted its occurrence with pre-rational clairvoyant accuracy. Nobody died. But there was a plot. But there are plots everywhere."

Anver stops me. "The untrained eye. I hadn't thought of the last one. The newspaper thing for a man of your stature and learning?"

For some strange reason, I see myself as a younger man in an aircraft descending over a city with sand all around it. Clearly, I am landing in the most loveless city in the Middle East: Cairo. *El Kairaya-El-Ma'ha'russa*—the well-guarded city. Someone from the flight crew announces the descent in Arabic, English, and German. So I must have boarded the flight in Frankfurt.

"Are you writing a book, or are you a cop? Be straight with me, please. Who are you? Or are you Anver playing old-age drama class with me?"

The world expert on banalities can't compete with an old man. "I am not a cop. I am writing a book. It is not a documentary. Fiction or nearly fiction." Linda has heard bits and pieces, I'm sure. Doesn't scare me.

I'm in the common room with red leather chairs and those windows that place the little river-lake dead centre. I focus my attention on three branches. There's a wind. No leaves. Three branches. I think I hear the sound of rain throughout the conversation that is transpiring beside me, not really beside me but a few red leather chairs down. The floors are shiny, as usual. A cleaner is using that electric floor shiner down the hall. I can hear it—sandpaper on marble. What a pleasure it is.

What day is it? Vernal something or another? Ash Wednesday? All Saints Day? Or Saint Patrick's? Palm Sunday? Doesn't matter, I suppose. Tatjana marks time like this. Religion equals time for her. But for me, time is marked off by this: last week our population shrank by five: Mr. Overall, room 401— didn't know him very well—had a very final heart attack; he had endured several, Linda told me. I am not allowed to mention names; room 444 contained a total kidney failure, and something else that leads to death. Ms. Fishnet Stockings in 220 west-wing: heart attack terribly final. The tranquil saint in room 200 west-wing experienced a firecracker aneurysm, and the wheelchair art historian finally ran out of battery power. I think he stopped on the word, "Cézannnn." The tall dark stranger from room 411 had a fall down only two steps. Skull fractures to infinity. Hardly any legal complications for the residence, because his son had taken him off residence property, on a visit, on the town. Bustling downtown Pierrefonds, Québec. The son looked very guilty, but wasn't. I saw him when he was here to pick up his father's things. "Sorry about your dad," I say. Cellular death in key organs. I felt like asking him if he had pushed to get the money. But that would not have been nice.

He thanks me for my sympathy. His father had not been in good shape. The son had turned around for a minute and his father had fallen. The cops took the son's side. The exact amount of money transferred to his account is a matter that Linda will tell me about. We have a deal.

30

Silver platter

For image reasons, nurses don't wear white coats anymore. I saw them giving Mrs. Mulroney a bath when I was walking past room 312 in the eastern side of the home. Why was the door ajar? Her flesh hung in thin translucent gills below her armpits. She groaned at each passing of the shower head. The water was steaming. Dead grey look. Why does the body still keep breathing and eating? Why not just a firm goodbye? These mean thoughts come not only to me—others admit to having had them. Mrs. Gills has another two weeks, not a nanosecond more. So bathe her in fragrant oils, and rub musk on her skin and bury her by the silent stones where the night winds whisper. She saw me. I looked right back. Sympathetic, my look? Not at all. Dead neutral, pardon the pun.

Was a genetically predetermined programme going to turn her into a dolphin? Chromosome aberrations? Who was going to receive her e-mails? Does she even get any? Will Linda let me see her mail? What would I read? Letters from a blonde daughter in Sarnia? Twin sons in Markham? Speaking of e-mails, I should look at mine, one of these days.

Life becomes a stream of questions. But then why flirt at seventy years of age or whatever age I am? Why not?

What am I supposed to do? Why does the dead banker's wife's daughter have the movements and the sounds of old age?

"Is she going to visit me this afternoon?" Tatjana asks out loud.

"I think so; our nurse was mentioning it."

Linda is about to leave after giving me my four o'clock: "Oh yeah, that detective called again. Notice how I'm not sticking my nose in your affairs?" She laughs as she moves out of the door frame; I guess she knows that Anver is playing theatre with me.

"Okay, I'll call him now. Like my efficiency? Pass me the phone please." Anver up to his old drama.

I sip brandy, clear my throat and look out at the river. Which season have we gone through? One of the four. Which direction are we moving in? Spring or fall? I can't tell. She was just giving me my five o'clock. And now its summer on a silver platter, and a few newspaper hounds are calling me. Fame, flattery after all these years of degenerative changes.

31

Your humble servant

Six months have passed. Linda tells me six years. Perhaps two years. Tatjana knows what a toothbrush is. Due to the pills. Next she'll know what a butterfly is. Blueberry pills for memory improvement; usually four to six to bring back memory. Latest thing. She regains her memory, and I am not sure what is happening. The pills and I have helped her. I remind her of things and what they do. Linda congratulates me for being so helpful: we've become deep, committed friends. Tatjana can now, because of me, remember about forty objects of every one hundred previously forgotten. She is forgetting less and less. I can see the walls making compartments in her mind.

No. I'm not in love with anyone in this old folks home. Now, I must take a look at my mail. Letters, a few letters. Now, let's see again, one e-mail to the wrong Dr. Joseph Macleod. Coincidence that this old fogies' home has two John Macleods and both are doctors.

People will do anything to stop from going crazy in here. Toothbrushes, dolls, dog skulls? Pierrefonds will do that to the best among us. I play postman. I hand-deliver the printed e-mail to him in room 360. View of a small road outside his window. Linda and I had a laugh over it all. I speak loudly and slowly: "Hello Doctor

Macleod, how are you? More misdirected e-mails. I have a letter for you. What can we do with this problem: our addresses keep getting crossed."

He looks attentively at me then slowly: "Good you came. I've a postcard for you; it's the old kind with a stamp, from somewhere in the States. I didn't read it, of course."

He's confident that I, too, have respected his privacy. I gently hand over the printed letter. I bid the old man a nice day and return to my room, postcard in hand.

An unsent e-mail oozes up. To: my lost lover. I'll send it one day, in the very near future—or perhaps I'll never send it. But I will. It is in my nature somehow. I like unambiguous starts like this. And I can't tell Linda anything about this, because that would be going too far. In my room, I look at my computer screen.

From: Joseph M to

My Dearest,

I love you. We left each other. Various versions, but yours is the most truthful. One can never expect to be pardoned for having lost some of the initial desire for you. I still love you. There is a reason. It will be easier to see where things lie if I say it all directly. I want very much to continue to see you. There are only a few years left, if that. Can you please call me?

I think that with all our past intimacy, we can bring a different friendship into some kind of fruition that will not hurt you in any way. This is presumptuous, I know; but do you want me to live without hope? I know it will take emotional skill for you to see me. I need you as a friend. I need you deeply. Those years with you meant very much to me. How much our mornings meant for me. Day-to-day things.

Sorry, I don't know how to avoid the maudlin tone. I've broken into a desperate desire to write to you, to try to see you again, as a close friend. Who is he kidding? you might be saying. How are our sons Ian and Michael? They must be tall beautiful men by now. Can you send me a photograph? I didn't think so. I knew our separation was forever. I am sorry. The day before the angels take me, I'll push "send," and you'll get this e-mail, and then the world will know. Know what? My contribution to history was not much. I was the only one in the game who didn't kill any donkeys.

Joseph, your humble servant.

32

No brothers. No sisters. No children

Someone from the home has lent me a car. I am visiting Linda in Montreal. Did I rent the car, or is it true that someone from the home lent it to me? Linda lives in a middle-class neighbourhood near a park. I take an elevator up some floors. I pull my hand out of my pocket, take off my glove, put the glove back into my pocket, and then a few thoughts flash through my head: Have I been to this part of Montreal before? I think I used to live in this neighbourhood. The elevator stops; I walk out and face a hallway as long as an underground train in Hong Kong. But there aren't any high-rise apartment buildings near here. Where am I? I knock. She opens the door.

"Never seen you with your hair down before. No. You had you hair down at the home; last Monday, if I remember correctly—remember you—you remember you're going to say."

"Any difficulty finding the place?"

"Came right here. I parked the car a few blocks away because I wanted to walk. I think I lived in this area. Has the concept of *Monday* become one of those faded days?"

"You'll have a scotch I know. You're not sure you lived in this area?"

"Thank you. A scotch, yes. Seems like I forget things, but they've come back to me. I am glad you're around this kind of group memory loss. Gives me confidence in our friendship."

I look into the apartment from the door.

"So this is where you live. Thank my lucky stars you have abstract paintings. I get fed up with living with all those hillbilly landscapes in our home in Uricville. They try to look so modern. Let me move in with you. I know I'm very handsome, and don't worry, I won't tell the home about our meeting. Not unless you take your clothes off right now."

She puts my coat on a hanger and slips it into the closet. Please, have a seat. A pause follows. I sip the scotch looking down at the Afghan carpet. I recognize things immediately: Kandahar. And, then, another sip.

"Well, Dr. Macleod, we certainly have an understanding, don't we?"

"Understanding?"

"I love your company. Is that too simple to be reasonably acceptable? Do tell me if that is the case."

"One wonders. Pleasure in each other's company? Youth and aged beauty."

My niceness toward Linda works. She invites me to her apartment for tea again and again. Youth needs age.

"I can still drive. Someone lent me a car. Lucrece's daughter? It's someone's car that I'm driving. Is it mine?" This makes her laugh. Electra complex? Doubt it. You see, I am not overweight, so it's not surprising she would not be repulsed by me. Sort of an upper-middle-class neighbourhood.

"I almost did not recognize you, I've never seen you with your hair down before," I say.

"Come in." As usual, she helps me with my coat.

"You're having less and less difficulty getting here, I hope."

"Came right here. I parked the car a few blocks away, because I wanted to walk."

"Would you like something to drink?"

"Scotch not run out, has it?"

"Are you sure you want something that strong?"

"Yes. Please." Our conversation wanders. She is not nosy at all. Even though she had heard rumours. It was me and my knowledge of things that made her want to while away six or more afternoons with me. Would I like something to drink? She'd always ask. Just a touch, I would say, always. She can have my money if she wants it: I've no one in my life at the moment. My visits go on a few more times, then we take a break for a year. Don't know why. A lover she had? I did not miss her. But when I started to see her again at her house, the pain of not having seen her made me cry. She held me in her arms. I have told her everything about my life, and why I love returning to this part of Montreal. And, yes, I can leave you a shitload of money when I die. I already met with my lawyer. I've no one else to leave it to. No brothers. No sisters. No children.

At times during the day here, I see myself in my past, or perhaps its my past self that intrudes in my peace by the river. Should I share this panparahistoricism with Linda? I will in due time. My newspaper clippings read me in my favourite chair, black leather, newsprint reflected brightly in my glasses.

My Dearest fellow murderer,

Am I wrong to assume that you'd love me forever? Is there some cruel arrogance in saying this? But doesn't this recognition mean that I've always loved you or that I've recognized in seeing your love for me a longevity in us? How else can I explain this historic attachment to you after all these years? Not a single day without you in my life in those years that passed in your apartment beside a park with the dark, curly-haired Italians training for the World Cup. There is not a single day that I don't think about you. There will never be a day without you. Will you ever forgive me for not desiring you as much as I did in the beginning? You must find a way to forgive me. Why won't you find a way to forgive me?

I want to see you every day. But how the cold winds blow. Are you sure you can't make a little room for me in your life? Life is so short. Please. Please? Will it really be too painful for you to make a little room? Maybe the pain will go away. Are you scared that things in this context will be superficial and meaningless? But we are in our seventies now. You don't know how much I wanted to age with you. But how could I have lived with you? A ridiculous question. You've seen how I ended up, haven't you? I dreamed that you came to see me when I was sleeping. I was watching them play cricket; cricket is another word for terrorism.

Constant aloneness, that's what I have now in this last stop: long emphasis on the nessssssssss. Must try to make you laugh; that way you'll remember. Am I being mean in expressing my desire? I see depth to us. Nice music we listened to. Even though you claimed to have full understanding of it. Of course, I could only understand it partially.

A love that never dies. Can you please reach me?

With reverence,
yours,
Joseph

I show and discuss the above letter with Linda. It brings us together. We're walking outside the home, on a narrow stony beach around the tiny lake.

"I get the impression, I get the impression that you need to know more—about me, I mean if we are to remain friends. You should."

"We're going to remain friends, yes. There's nothing nosy about me wanting to know what happened in your past life, is there?"

"I don't think you're nosy. Yes, I organized the London trauma—big word for such a small series of things. You're not shocked, are you? I've willed your silence, and you're in my will. Deathbed confession. That's what you're getting, without the deathbed. Is it legal to promote hate against a people—Moslems? My object was to frighten the European chancelleries—scare the sausages out of them."

"Noble. Can they do anything now?"

"There is nothing the authorities can do now. They can't base a trial on the diaries of one of the fools I hired. You have difficulty accepting who I am and why the playing field is not even."

"What if he testifies against you in court? What government gave you money to do this?"

"He? Who? Court? Proof? Governments? Crap. Three of my fellow organizers are in this home now. Things aren't how they appear, are they? We are years down the line. In fact, I am sure that that's the bastard who wants information—has been calling so often. Maybe he really is a writer, as he says he is. Fucked if I know. Why did I do it? Political convictions enveloped in the desire to get rich—is that what you think? But mostly to get rich quick. Most TV westerners think there isn't any money in terrorism. But there is. You heard part of the conversation with Anver, or was it someone else? I get confused. You know I get confused."

"Who paid you? Hey, why don't I write your life story? Then I could get rich as well. You make things up, don't you?"

"A rich regime paid me—Damascus, Teheran, Islamocosmomondo. An Arab regime, an enlightened Arab country, that's how the world saw it. What does it matter now which regime paid? Don't worry. Who paid Thatcher—the Queen of Western Terrorocotta? Are you sure you want to know who paid? Are you working for Old

Folks Homeland Security? I am about to die in the next few months—the government—a Middle Eastern country, which has 349 days of sunshine. How's my disease? What did the doctors say: what's the report?"

"Can't really tell until we get the results. Wish we had more sunshine here. You've several years to live. In theory. Which country was it?"

"I don't care about the results. I'm not suffering. I can't feel it eating away. The pills work wonders."

"Any regrets?"

"Regrets? What's that? Explain the concept. What's that?"

"Who was Gorgana?"

"Never heard of her."

"Was she Usha? Tatjana? Someone else?"

"I don't understand. You tell me. Who was Gorgana?"

33

Ezekiel 44.7

I've walked over to Anver's room. I sit down beside him and look out onto the river and lawn. I have to kill him: I think he is leaking. Poor fool doesn't know what is coming.

"We've had a good intelligence harvest," I say. He looks like he understands what I've said. We're both old, yes, but we're in the ultra-modern era for aging. Eighty equals an athletic sixty with or without bladder cancer.

I'm sure that somehow Anver, while eating pig fat, is leaking information to journalists. But then again I am not sure. I can't be a hundred percent sure but somehow, he could show the world what we did. And what are the consequences of the exposure? Nothing much. We are going to paradise within the next five years. How to fix this? I want to tell him that I agree that we should do a geezer operation—just a last one—and we could conduct it on a small synagogue or a place that makes gravestones for Jewish clients.

"Anver, should we do one last one?"

"What? You changed your mind?"

"I was thinking of that place near rue Mordechai Vanunu, in the Plateau area of Montreal—you know the place that makes those gravestones. Why don't we do our last operation together?" I say.

"Why don't we get Water, Electricity and/or Sanitation?"

"We don't have money to do much except something old-fashioned and cheap. I can promise you the standard thermoluminescence, but with much lighter material than we used to use—the new stuff is like walking in with a paper envelope—bang to the bastards. We're gainfully employed again. Happy?"

"I don't mind; glad you're into this—what do we do?"

Linda comes in and says hello. Does either of us need anything or is everything ok in here?

"All is well with us. Thanks. Linda, today I am eighty-five." Linda smiles and leaves, and we continue planning.

"We have some supplies—all modern stuff—we put it right inside, you pretend you're going to buy a large gravestone for a relative."

"But the last name on my ID is not something Berg. And Anver is not too correct-sounding, is it? What do you suggest I say when I'm placing the order? And how big is the thing and does it have enough pop?"

"Say it's for Hymiebergsteingoldandsilverberg—that should cover all the bases. And, yes it does have enough power to bring the hidden Imam into view."

"How did you get such a pop machine? But that's a long last name, isn't it?"

"Do you want to do something or not? Order two with the Hebrew inscriptions—something from Ezekiel—perhaps Ezekiel 44.7 and use your credit card."

"Are you sure? My credit card? Anver Mohammad on my credit card? Joseph, you make me laugh. And what if one of us gets injured? They'll trace it back to the home, won't they?"

"Use cash. They'll ask for a down payment. Give them cash. Credit card later on."

"But no one knows what cash is. This is not professional. How do we pay? Can we pay later? I mean, they'll take months to chisel out *Bergsteingoldsilver.*"

"Yes. Months. Causing death is professional. I think they have machines to carve in the words."

"Ok, Joseph. We'll do one last one terrorist event before we get to heaven."

"No sign of getting caught yet. I don't suppose they will catch us now, do you?"

"So here's the summary: Tuesday, we do a walk-by but don't order anything. Friday we walk past, then walk back, then walk in and order stones from them. Then on Sunday 3 November, during the city elections, we do it."

"But the gravestone-making place is right beside the kindergarten," Anver says.

"Well, then it'll be a good day for the kiddies."

"Let's change it to Monday then?"

"Ok, we'll do it Monday—but that way we don't get to interrupt the city elections, do we?"

"You can't get everything you want. Do you want some kids or do you want to screw up the city elections? The owner of this gravestone place sends money to Israel, which makes graves, not gravestones. Anyway, if you want kids, then we do it Friday.

When we do the ordering we can leave the pop device, much smaller than the earlier days. The person taking the order will not notice that we're leaving something. We'll do this when we are being given a tour of how the shop makes the stones for the dead. So we walk in, have a general chat with them. Tell them we'd like to see where the work is done, out-of-interestism. They will show us their workshop. When they look away we leave the bomb. We walk out. Then a few seconds later. Bang goes the weasel: Article 22 of the 1961 Vienna convention on Diplomatic Relations."

"Who are the diplomats? The kids belong to diplomats?"

"Yes, the kids are extensions of the diplomats."

Our raillery continues but soon ends.

On Friday we catch the train at Lucien-L'Allier, then we get off at Lionel Groulx and continue on the Green Line in the direction of Honoré-Beaugrand. We get off at St. Laurent and take the 55 Bus north to Napoleon. I ask my lifelong friend Anver to walk over to the gravestone makers and past the kindergarten. He does this; he has no idea I am going to push the buttons on my cellphone. A nostalgic yellow-white flash arches up in a pure S form, then a pure white light performs yet another S shape in the afternoon sky. S is the complex conjugate of S. And then a nostalgic bang: I have my Islamic ear protectors on, so I feel nothing at all. The gravestones, now light as light as birds, fly upward into the sky, seeming to following the smoky S curve and land directly on him. I thought I just heard a squish sound, but I didn't. I have my Islamic hearing protectors on.

That evening the reports say several were killed and blah blah and the remains of an older man, who through Allah's mercy and my timing, was destroyed beyond recognition. His departure from this world was attributed, not to the blast, but by being crushed by two gravestones falling directly on his head and shoulders from the Christian sky. The stones for Silverberg and Goldberg were the heavy birds who came home to roost on poor Anver's shoulders, head, and ribcage all crushed beyond belief. An innocent old man, simply walking past the grey gravestones. Of course, the bleeding kids from the kindergarten next door were enough to make me feel guilty but only for a few seconds. As the kids are being taken to the hospital by noisy ambulances, I start to think about the kids in Kabul. The Saint Urbain bus takes me to the home for aged, successful terrorists. I thought I heard a kid's arm fly off into the cosmological yonder, but an arm hasn't a mouth so it must have been my imagination. From the bus window, I can see a baby's talking arm following the bus, but this must be RTG—routine temporary guilt. I have so much guilt. One of the kids was the son of a blue chip diplomat, so we fulfilled our commitment as set out in the Vienna Convention—one bird, a few gravestones—a fist in the dam of idle conversation. Milquetoast we're not.

34

Milt Jackson on the River Ravi

I put on some music from my childhood: John Lewis on piano, Milt Jackson on vibes, Percy Heath playing bass, Connie Kay drums, the Modern Jazz Quartet, a little something called "That Slavic Smile." It will last 8:01 minutes. At 5:23 minutes into this masterpiece, John Lewis' hands will hit an octave, Milt Jackson will play a few sequences acknowledging his historical masters, the great black and white blues men of the Delta; and the piece will flow into a whimpering tender ending. These musicians have all been dead since the last century.

I replay "That Slavic Smile." At exactly 5:23 minutes into the song, and on an octave, I sit down and open a drawer near my bed. After placing a fluorescent blue pill of Viagra One on my tongue, I swallow some water and put the glass down on my white bedside table and continue slowly walking around Tatjana Lucrece's sleeping body. Every year, they come up with a newer, better version—next year it'll be Viagra Two—and more expensive. Pharmaceutical bastards prey on us aged, as we prey on time.

The new and advanced memory pills tell me that I remember sex. The Viagra tells me I still have a willy. Memory plus engorged penis equals Tatjana Lucrece. Seems rudimentary. I am rudimentary, but the world around me is more so. Icebergs are rudimentary.

Milt Jackson's vibes tinkle in my mind. The home is silent. Tatjana is sexually desirous of me: She wants me. Proof: She touched my hand once at dinner. Night descends as I walk down the aged hallway with medium-priced paintings by local, very local, talent. What could be worse than a hack who copies the impressionists? I've enough memory to know what impressionists are.

What if she is not feeling like a screw? I pass the kitchen in a mood of sexual over-confidence. Priapic. No cluttering pots and pans, and I am not listening to the water evaporate off the tips of forks, knives and spoons. No donkeys from the Arab world wandering in the kitchen. Male and female food servers in light green gowns—where are they? Glorious, dark silence. I love the quiet of the home at night. However, there's the question of the blithering telephone, which one can hear if one tries. In the background a nurse chats into the phone. I think I hear the word "Mohammad." Of course I ignore it, thinking that it would take too much recall strength to attach a face to the word sounds.

Tatjana's left her door ajar, or was it the nurse? If she remembers anything, I'll say Tatjana and I cut a deal. What's the administration going to say? At any rate, I am, providentially, in her room. There's a small light in the electrical socket and the curtains have been left open. Enough light enters so that I can see a clear outline of her body and face. Tiptoeing toward the bed, I watch her sleep, her face-wrinkles drooping to the floor. Nurse Linda gave me the pills. Saint Salt Peter the patron saint of droop. And no, they don't put it in our food. Tatjana is beautiful from where I stand. My love for her is as deep as it was for Usha, because we understand each other. Usha, that drinker of Earl Grey, that scenter of rooms, that personalizer of unpersonalizable rooms, was my best friend in the western part of the home.

Peacefully, she lies in a soft object called sleep. Why has she forgotten about sex? Has she? How do I know this? Does her bed have wheels on it? No, a normal bed; she's not that sick yet. Usha: alive one minute, prattling on with stories about Cairo, Oncle Ibn Maurice, the mosque of Ibn Tulun, the next silence. Thin-lipped Usha—whose lips I once touched after breakfast. Usha, the bird woman who called starlings to the window, just to prove she could do it. And they came: effusive starlings, flapping, waking up the entire home like a noisy parliament of old birds.

My heart is not stone. I could feel the pain of Usha's death, but when you've passed the seventy-nine-year mark, you get too old to feel things as you may have once. You become too old even to get cancer. So when one loses a loved one as it is referred to, one does not suffer as much as one used to. The pain has never lasted more than a few minutes, simply because our brains can't remember what to get upset about. Death and departure are made into human exaggerations so funeral homes will make money. The grief industry makes coffins out of gold, patients entombed at –320 degrees, waiting to be reanimated (re-Mohammadized) in 2090 or whenever our specialists can invent something that will make them more money. Notice the cardinal strength of that number seventy-two?

Usha's death caused me no pain. None at all. Guess how many of my last friends here have died? I've seen five die in one week—all great friends they had become—they all died because their cells no longer had that replicative capacity to conduct operations. Doctors, please let us die in peace, please. Five deaths in a week is a record in the Death by Terror Olympics. Five homicide bombers and their controllers all live here. Fuck you all.

Heart of stone? No, I don't have a heart of stone. Heart of no memory—one has to have memory to feel. I have a heart that remembers, and those pills that fix the effects of the "oxygen paradox." They invent a new term every two minutes—I'll be able to get emotionally hurt very soon because my Aberrant Telomeres are no longer fading away.

Near the bed, under the cover of night, a fan blows indolent summer air across her breasts, de-oxidizing them. She ages less in the artificial wind. That's something the experimental doctors might say. I really do hear them saying things like that. The blanket is covered in moonlight below her waist. Can she feel my breathing along her neck wrinkles? Is she dead? I don't think so. The Alzheimer-Necrophilia-Geezer-Rapist strikes again—well, for the first time.

Under the sable night of dread and fear, I move toward her. Bet she can't feel my breathing as my hand moves up her thigh. The Viagra has me on autopilot. Right on. In my mind's ear, I can hear geezer rock-and-roll music: the Rolling Stones, Van Morrison, Jim Morrison ... I see guitars smashing on a stage. "People are strange when you're a stranger." Will Linda forgive me? I am only fucking her in the pineal gland, nothing more than that, is it? Will Linda forgive me? Forgive me for what? Has she encouraged me? Indirectly, I mean. Can she be blamed for this? Yes, she can be blamed. Very directly. I'm not doing anything Tatjana would not want me to do, am I? She held my hand. Besides, who will forget first, Tatjana or me? She'll forget first. She forgets things that have not happened, that's how bad her condition is. Bet she can't remember two sentences after she starts to complain to the nurse. The morning after. Complain of what? Had an itch when I woke up. Not my fault. Consenting adults. Consenting free radicals that eat up the memory cells. Hence we age, like wanton boys; the oxygen molecules kill us for sport. Though Tatjana has periods for weeks in which she has normal long-term and short-term memory.

The warm wind cools in rhythmic sections. I haven't taken any Viagra, that was a cool lie. Cool here, as I step closer, warmer there. She stirs, feathered wings folded: listlessly, an arm arches over her white forehead, which is in a patch of moonlight. Her nose is beautifully long. Can she pull herself out of her sleep? I found it difficult to pull my mind from that dream I had during our Atlantic crossing, on that large ocean liner with those two Middle Eastern idiots who worked with us—who live with me now, in this home. I've not introduced them to her. What difference will it make whether or not she knows? What's the role of pleasure in all this?

A night owl settles on a tree nearby, my only witness. I see the dark Atlantic outside. Gulls screeching, little innocent fish in their mouths. The waves crash against the boat. Stiff as a man of eighteen and lubed up with something, don't know what it is. She is rattled awake by a falling spoon from the bedside table. I'm beside her, and gently, ever so gently she oozes out of her peaceful sleep into my Viagrian reality.

"Hello, Joseph, what are you doing here? Late isn't?"

I thought she'd want me to come to visit. That's why I came. She does not sense the aggression: of course there is none. That's just the chemicals taking control. I think she falls back asleep. She called me by my name. The tension vanishes. Then she asks, what are you doing here, in my room? She pushes against me and raises her voice, slightly. But I persist, I mean, my hands persist. I snuggle under the blankets. She offers more resistance, then just like in Hollywood films she kisses my neck, her withering body fully igniting at age eighty-something-something. Her thighs slowly slide up in between my legs; every second of skin contact is paradise for me. I touch her waist and bury my nose in her neck. There is a smell of a child in old people. Piss, the universal solvent follows us to from the cradle to the near-grave. Tenderly, I part her legs. She says she doesn't want to. Why not? Why don't you want to? But why is she holding me like this if she doesn't want to? She is breathing deeply. Will the shock of penetration kill her? Dream on old boy—there is no Viagra, no stiff penis. But I continue dreaming that waves of sperm froth into her. Dream on. Fertile as hell they must all be, singing "Under My Thumb" upstream to impregnate eggs tumbling down her fallopian tubes. We are in a deep cuddle, flesh contact brings us together. She calls out her late husband's name, Ben, oh Ben, Ben Habib, I never thought you'd come back. Oh my God, she's missed two periods. Dream or reality? Again and again, her head moves back and forth in pleasure. Old people are much younger now than they used to be. I tell her it's Joseph, Joseph from down the hall. She clues in for a second time and holds me closer to her. I put my head down on her breasts. I'm in love again. Usha is a faded memory. The scent of childhood merges with the star-filled Atlantic.

Her body smells of subtle, expensive perfume—which smells mainly of rose, an occasional echo of garlic salami ending with a preponderance of lavender and fox bladders. I ask her if I can give her a birthday gift of 747 jet fume perfume. Tatjana says that being with me is wonderful. She recalls our conversation about my visit. Thanks for coming, she says, laughing. Again, she pulls me toward her. I almost forget that you said that you were going to come tonight. I've now become aware of her perfume: it is guilty—daughter perfume. I pull her into my arms. I notice that she has had a partial mastectomy—ductal carcinoma it must have been; or is my anatomy off again? Also, I see a small scar that a lumbar puncture has left. She is flesh, and she's warm. She likes me. The tips of my fingers find the healed scars. We fall into a coma. Three hours later, the spinning earth wakes me: with the rustling of bed sheets, she awakes too. I say I'll be off to my room before everyone in the home wakes up. She pulls me down onto her sagging flesh trying to let me undo the bond. Shaky hands, rosy lips. I affectionately resist her tug, and tell her I must leave, reminding her that her daughter is visiting first thing today. She remembers and in her sand-and-spit old lady's voice, says:

"Ah! you're right. Yes, today, Do you want to say hello to her again?"

"Well, yes, I do want to see her again. I'll come by after you two have had a chat, shall I?" I get out of bed to leave.

She bursts into tears. "Please don't leave me. It felt so good to have you near my side. I love having your body beside mine. I'm so lonely, I've forgotten what loneliness is."

The early morning birds have begun their chirping; mechanically, a programmed fog meanders over the indolent wog-filled River Ravi beside our home. The owl is not real: it's there to scare the pigeons away. An eternity in wood. She's on her elbow on the bed, hips elegantly arched like spring meadows, tears draining down her cheeks, which I kiss again and again. She holds my hand. I shuffle out. Softly yet firmly with trembling voice, she calls out: "Joseph don't leave me now, stay with me, I haven't been with anyone in many years. Joseph, I'm not dreaming this, don't leave me, don't. Please."

What she can't remember will not sadden her. With my back to her, I leave smiling victoriously, an endless gully of tears in my wake.

35

Late-Camel Linear B

Is it true that Usha has a fistula between the rectum and the bladder? Fecal matter in her urine? Abnormal passage? Damn right: rectovesical fistula. Who has ulcerative colitis? Crohn's disease—someone near me has it. Or was it rectal tuberculosis? Where am I in this time distortion? Do I need a sigmiodoscope to know where I am? A sigmiodoscope is a more curious anoscope. I've experienced both, sometimes with pleasure. But all this will not help me locate myself spatially. All I really want to know is when I got here, here in Linda's apartment.

I'm back in my nurse's apartment, high up, overlooking the mountain. For an instant, one of the small cars below catches my attention. Who lent me the car to get here? Did someone lend it to me to get here? Did they drive me? Who?

The frost on the windows has formed leafy patterns. Minus 20 degrees centigrade and falling. Linda sees me trace the lines in the leafy patterns with my fingers. How has the humidity in here transformed into such beautiful leaves? I follow a particular tributary of one of the larger frost leaves. I find a smaller rivulet, then a smaller one, then an even smaller one, and after that, I follow a series of dots of frost. I realize that there are no longer any detectable frost particles. The remaining sunlight throws the smallest bits of frost into mountainous relief, like Greenland seen from an airplane during a sunset on the way to a bombing. Pink, with deep blue out there. The immaculate conception of leaves would happen tomorrow, temperature and humidity permitting. It's an afternoon in February. A stream of cold cars flows north along Avenue du Parc toward rue Mont-Royal.

What I have just given you is a florid physicalist equivalent of a mechanical world. As things get smaller, the fundamental rules change. There was only one scientist here that I could talk to, but he's got a disease. He says that there is an entire world at ten to the minus thirty-three metres or centimetres in a superposition and lots of arrows instead of numbers ↑↓↑↓↑↓, where state vectors get entangled, and a throbbing spin of 0, ½, 1, or 3/2, 2 depending on the afternoon, depending on the century, depending on which theory has been turned to myth by the imminent arrival of the future—which he'd say, just arrived. See, we were just in the past. He made me into a cosmologist and a quantum mechanical terrorist/healer-against-imperialismosis.

He did not believe in God, the only thing right with him. Hail Mary full of Grace, pray for me. Hail Memory stored below gluons, quarks, charmed quarks, fermions. The unseen particles don't encourage God. Encourage? What could that possibly mean? We see the word "encourage" written on a piece of paper, which itself consists of smaller and smaller particles. The black ink makes us think of an image: the image is stored in the brain which itself is made up of other particles. Particles all the way down. Now why can't I remember his name today, or yesterday or the day before: lack of particles? Can't be that, I've lots of particles. He's been taken out of circulation. He's in a bed, green curtain to his side, bit of sunlight. I walked past his room. No life left, merely oxygen going into his lungs, which are themselves made of smaller and smaller particles. Heavy helium. An indolent South Asian breeze flows out of his nostrils.

I sit. I wait for Rabi' al-thani to flow into Jumada al-awwal while thinking that quantum mechanical terrorism can be done only in the English language. One certainly can't do it in Arabic, Urdu, Spanish, even German. What kind of mathematical descriptions of the world would we get with Late-camel Linear B?

What came first, fur or feathers? My friends have fluttered off. Now I have fewer friends. None left in London. None left in Toronto, except my brother and his wife. And an aged aunt in Peterborough, Ontario. No one visits. I am an atheist among believers, with their expensive and shiny crucifixes on sable cashmere sweaters worn by the wives of dead bankers. Merry Wives of Pierrefonds, dying in splendour.

Jumada al-thani. Twilight. No river in front of my room. I must be in Linda's high-rise: she's gone on holidays and has given me the keys to her apartment. Why has she done this? We're just friends. But all the same, I do have keys. I come here to get away from the old folks home. Here, in her high-rise, I have a full view of Mount Royal Park's long hill covered in snow. Skeletal trees poke out of a blanket of snow. At night, I can see the crucifix: Our Cross with Electric Bulbs by Hydro Quebec—

glowing tribute to French-Canadian Catholic secularism. Montréal, Qom of the Western World. "Minus twenty and falling," I announce to everyone. Everyone? Just her and me. Like cows, the old folks look up at me and they clap, sarcasm being the furthest thing from their mental skills. Iqbal Masoume, more aged than I, asks: "What's for supper?" Sammy, at the card table, less aged than I, replies: "Why worry about what's for supper? We just had breakfast twenty minutes ago." Aging away in splendour.

Rajab. The red-lipsticked wives of bankers, insurance company presidents, and even richer bankers nod, pretending that they know what literary agents are. The poor die differently. We tried to prevent all that, but somehow we've ended up in this place for the rich? Who is paying for us? There are some educated women here, yes. One, in fact, Jennifer, was a literary agent. Brainy. Died last week. Another was a head librarian at one of the larger universities. She is still alive, in perfect health. She likes dietary fibre, used to knit sweaters made from these fibres. I love talking with her: she did a book, *The Fate of Libraries in War Zones*. After the people have been killed, the books and documents get it. They can't rebuild society because the blueprint has been blown away. She tells me of a librarian from Kosovo who was filmed with the public library burning in the background. Tears running down his face.

Jennifer's tall, has thin white hair, wears a baggy brown skirt and a white shirt. She has a memory that lasts four seconds and I had a yen for her. She asks the same questions, makes the same pronouncements, like an old card catalogue. She is a complete and utter stranger to me.

She takes a friendly step toward me. Jennifer, how do you do this afternoon? I'm Joseph. Dr. Joseph Macleod. Remember. How's your bone cancer? Remember you have brain cancer, not bone cancer. Spreading, is it? Iatrogenic, is it? I hope so. The doctor gave it to you? That's what they all say. Or was it bone cancer? I bet you've forgotten my name. Again. If you die, then I will not have to tell you my name every day, will I?

"Hello. Jennifer. How. Are. You. Today?"

"Hello. Mr. Saltmarsh, I'm fine. And how are you?"

The short-wave radio in my possession for centuries crackles with the incomprehensible voices of newsreaders. She looks at the radio in my hand; she smiles and waddles off down the hall. Saltmarsh—who's he? Must be me. That's the new me. Saltmarsh Me is from the future—her memory is so good that she forgets things from the future. How many Jennifers were there? Two: Jennifer remembers remembering Jennifer. Jennifer was a production assistant on the Tribeca affair. She became a close friend for two decades, and now I'm just another bunch of particles floating by. Any chance she'll reveal us to the authorities? I don't think so, she's post-revelationary with a lissom form. Can she tell the difference between the authorities, nurses and the cold-blooded killers we used to be? Who, in the widest sense of the word, isn't a bomber? My name is not John Macleod but Javid Mohammad or something like that. Sorry about my secretive side. I'm a non-state actor, who is, to this day, unconvicted, thus as innocent as all the others. I didn't mean to offend anyone.

P.S.:

Usha had super heavy periods which could be contained by the use of heavy-flow jam rags. The pharmacy where she used to buy them refused to stock them. The owner told her that only Moslems bled heavily or something equally terrorist. Usha, remember, was Irish. Well, we bombed that pharmacy at the exactly the same time —18:32—an Itwār AH something something as we bombed an art opening for a massive exhibition of the Group of Seven. Local artists loved our act because these institutions actively excluded their works; the act gave us Canadian content which, unfortunately, we made ashen in a few seconds: anti-Canadian content. The paradox made us laugh. All of A.Y. Jackson and Tom Thompson as well as Emily Carr. (We didn't want to be accused of sexism *and* murder.) We killed forty-five (only); five (only) of whom were smug international curators from China and England. And, in cold blood, we murdered ten at the local drug store where they never had heavy-flow tampons due to Islam or something like that. Understandably, we did cause offence to the local authorities and families, but we didn't mean anything personal by doing this: I swear to the almighty that every bit of it was political.

Acknowledgements

The airport sections within *Radius Islamicus* was an original idea for a screenplay, *Persona Non*, conceived by my friend Abouali Farmanfarmanian; we both wrote this work. I have, with his permission, re-written and included a few pages from that work.

Manal Stamboulie, Michael Springate, Michael Neumann, Rana Bose, Abouali Farmanfarmanian, Dimitri Nasrallah, Ian McLachlan, Fred McSherry, Michael Ryan, Martin Dowding, Matthew Sanger, Tim Spring, Michel Giroux, Loren Edizel, Sean Kane, Benjamin Shear, Ricardo Sternberg, and Claudio Gaudio commented on my manuscript. If I fall under the eyes of the intelligence community my commentators ought to be implicated as well: I couldn't have finished the novel without their encouragement.

That my characters resemble anyone living or dead is absolute fiction.

The Québec Arts and Letters Council, the Writers' Trust of Canada, and the Ontario Arts Council: The Writer's Reserve gave me grants to complete this work on non-state actors.

About the Author

Currently residing in Toronto after living in Montreal for three decades, Julian Samuel is a writer, documentary filmmaker, and visual artist. Publications include a novel, *Passage to Lahore*, and poetry, *Lone Ranger in Pakistan*. He has directed many documentaries including: *The Raft of the Medusa: Five voices on colonies, nations and histories, Into the European Mirror, City of the Dead and the World Exhibitions, Save and Burn* and *Atheism*. His articles and essays have appeared in Canadian Literature and Fuse, Race and Class, The Montreal Gazette, Le Devoir, La Presse, Counterpunch, Books in Canada and Montreal Serai. *Radius Islamicus* is his second novel. For more information on Julian's past and recent work, check out his website, www. julianjsamuel.com.